MW01227189

# KILLER
## *Attraction*

# KILLER
## *Attraction*

## AVERY FLYNN

This book is a work of fiction. Names, characters, places, and incidents are the product of the author's imagination or are used fictitiously. Any resemblance to actual events, locales, or persons, living or dead, is coincidental.

Copyright © 2014 by Avery Flynn. All rights reserved, including the right to reproduce, distribute, or transmit in any form or by any means. For information regarding subsidiary rights, please contact the Publisher.

Entangled Publishing, LLC
2614 South Timberline Road
Suite 109
Fort Collins, CO 80525
Visit our website at www.entangledpublishing.com.

Ignite is an imprint of Entangled Publishing, LLC.

Edited by Stephen Morgan and Nina Bruhns
Cover design by L.J. Anderson
Cover art from iStock

Manufactured in the United States of America

First Edition May 2014

ignite

*For anyone who has ever feared adding a little color into their lives, but has done it anyway. Be brave. Be colorful. Be awesome.*

# Chapter One

*"One is never over-dressed or underdressed with a Little Black Dress."*

— KARL LAGERFELD

HARBOR CITY, NEW YORK

Paulie's Gym wasn't a fancy exercise emporium with spinning classes, personal trainers, and TVs hanging from the ceiling. The men and handful of women punching the heavy bag or trading jabs in the ring didn't care about those things. They came to work up a sweat, not gossip over the water cooler. No one cared that the smell was enough to knock a person on his ass, if his sparring partner's right hook didn't get him first.

Ignoring the sweat soaking through her black spandex tank top, Allegra "Ryder" Falcon balanced soft on her feet while people milled around outside the boxing ring. Her opponent had at least a hundred pounds on her, but she had something Cam Hardy didn't. Iron-willed focus…and the never-ending need to prove herself.

Locked in on her opponent, Ryder bounced on the balls of her feet, waiting for his attention to waver. All she needed was half a second to land a quick jab or high kick—

The gym door opened—

Cam's eyes shifted—

*Bam!* Ryder's right leg landed with a solid thump against his solar plexus.

Air wheezed out of his lungs like a fast deflating balloon.

She followed up with a quick punching combination and a roundhouse kick before grabbing his arm, spinning into position, and flipping him over her back.

He landed with enough force to make the ring's elevated floor bounce. Used to Ryder's weekly balls-to-the-wall sparring workouts, the other gym-goers barely glanced up from their own activities.

"Damn it Ryder," Cam mumbled around his mouth guard. "This is the last time I spar with you. The plan was to go easy on each other. Tony's right. You don't play well with others."

"You say that every time we spar, but you're still here twice a week without fail." She laughed and helped him up off the floor, which took considerably more effort than tossing him. "Man, have you gained weight?"

"Only muscle." He flexed his thick biceps as he shucked off the cushioned helmet, then winked one of his ice-blue eyes at her. "The ladies love it."

"Yeah, for the one night they get with you before you've moved on to the next unsuspecting sap." Cam's dating history was as long and sordid as a pornified version of *War and Peace*. If she didn't love him so much—like a second cousin twice removed—she'd punch even harder in the ring.

"Like you're any different. When was the last time I saw you with the same guy twice?"

That hit her right between the eyes. If Cam's fists connected as well as his words, she would have been the one on her ass. "I don't think my dates number anywhere near yours." She shrugged off the all-too-familiar ache. "Anyway, I have my reasons."

She had a type. Overly possessive, muscle-bound losers with a shaky grasp on employment and a too-tight grip on her. Then there was Heath. She shivered. He'd turned out to be even worse.

"Hey, the ladies enjoy themselves, and I never make any promises I can't keep." Cam put a foot on the ring's bottom rope and lifted the top one. "Speaking of which, how about you put in a good word about me with Drea?"

"Not in a million years." She slipped through the opening and stalked toward the locker room, leaving Cam and her bad memories behind her.

"How come?"

"One, she would eat you for breakfast. And two, I like Drea."

"You like me." Again, he winked.

How many girls had melted under Cam's patented charm offensive? Way more than she ever wanted to know about. "Not enough to sell out one of my best friends, pretty boy."

He laid his palm against his chest and mimed a faint. "You're killing me here."

"There's not a jury who would convict me." She pushed open the women's locker room's swinging door. "Especially since, with your dating history, at least half the jury would be made up of your ex-girlfriends."

God love the man, Cam was in for a world of hurt when he finally did find someone he wanted to be with for the long-term. Dude would not have any idea what to do. She couldn't wait to watch.

He reached out and gave her a noogie before she could

twist away. "Twenty-five is too young for you to be that damn cynical, Ryder girl. You know no woman is an island, not even you."

She shoved his hand away and stuck her tongue out. "So says the twenty-nine-year-old commitment phobe."

"Hey, we're not talking about me, here." There went that million-watt grin again.

"Cam, we're always talking about you." She patted his cheek. "And you love it."

The locker room door slammed shut behind her, and she peeled off her black workout clothes while ignoring the little voice reminding her of her own romantic mishaps. *Mishaps*. Now that was putting it mildly. More like a nuclear-level, chain-reaction explosion that gave her a nasty case of radiation poisoning so severe she could use her heart as a nightlight. For the entire tri-state area.

Ryder popped the handle on her locker right in time to hear the first buzz from her cell phone. The office number for Maltese Security flashed on the screen. As always, work rescued her from events she'd rather leave locked in a grimy basement.

She pressed the talk button. "*Hola*, boss, what's shaking?"

"I need you down at Dylan's Department Store right away." Tony Falcon, Maltese Security's owner, CEO, worrier-in-chief, and her big brother, had never been one for small talk, which just made Ryder want to needle him all the more.

"Hello to you, too, big brother. I'm doing great today, thanks for asking."

"Very funny. Dylan's is our biggest client right now. We can't afford for them to jump ship—not if I'm going to make payroll. I'm tied up on the Bowden case, and you're the only other one who's dealt with George Dylan before. He's quirky, but he likes you."

Ryder rolled her eyes. "He likes my ass." After their last

visit to Dylan's corporate headquarters, she was surprised she didn't have drool soaking the back of her black trousers. *Ewwww*.

"Ugh, you're my sister. Don't go there." Tony made a sound of disgust that reminded Ryder of her dog Kermit sucking the last bit of peanut butter from the roof of his mouth. "Here's the deal, someone has their hand in the company till. They need us to go in and figure out who and get the money back as quietly and quickly as possible. They're in the middle of a merger, and George is afraid if word leaks, the company's stock will tank and the deal will blow up."

Her pulse ratcheted up and she did a little jig. She was *so* in. "Sounds easy enough."

"Oh yeah, I'm sure everything will go off without a hitch." Sarcasm thickened her older brother's tone. "Even though I can't be there with you, I'll walk you through it every step of the way."

She slammed her locker door shut. "Tony, I have a degree in forensic accounting. You can barely balance your checkbook. I'm pretty sure I've got this."

"You're a funny girl, baby sister, but there's a big difference between book smarts and street smarts. Anyway, you go rogue on this like the last big case you had and I'll fire you faster than mom can dice a tomato."

Fighting the urge to scream with frustration, she closed her eyes and sucked in a deep breath. When she opened them a second later, the red haze had dissipated. "I grew up a cop's kid, just like you. I'm not some naif from the Midwest fresh off the bus." She paced in front of the lockers, already jonesing for another workout to blow off sibling-induced steam. "I can do this, Tony. Trust me."

"It's not that I don't—"

"Stop being my big brother and be my boss. You hired me. Do you think I can do the job or not?"

He didn't answer.

A lump the size of her Nonni's olive oil collection formed in her throat. She counted to five. If her phone had picked this moment to lose its signal, she was going to drown it in the toilet. "You there?"

"Yeah, I'm here." He sighed. "Okay, it's your case. Don't make me regret this. But you go over the plan with me. And you stay in contact with me while you're there."

"Yes, sir." She shimmied and almost tripped over her untied shoelaces.

Now, this sounded like a James Bond adventure—at least compared to the stalk-the-cheating-spouse shit she normally got assigned to as low chick on the totem pole. Add to that the fact that her family always treated her like she was still a ten-year-old tomboy in uneven pigtails and torn jeans, and it was enough to make her slam her head against the metal locker door. But this case could be her chance to prove them wrong and make them see her as she really was.

Forty-five quick minutes later, Ryder paused outside of George Dylan's office, her hand curled around the brass doorknob, eavesdropping on the very impassioned discussion happening on the other side of the thick oak doors. As the youngest of five kids, she'd perfected the skill while still in diapers. How else would she have gathered enough intel to blackmail her siblings into doing her chores? Lucky for Tony, she only used her powers for good these days.

Mostly.

The door muffled most of the conversation, but she managed to pluck a few phrases from the murmur.

"Don't need…" Something about the growly voice tugged on her memory.

"…A lid on it…" George Dylan's signature, two-pack-a-day wheeze identified the second speaker.

"Ruin everything…" Oh, mystery man was not thrilled

about bringing in professional help.

It wasn't the first time Maltese Security had run into client resistance on a case. Just like lawyers, no one wanted a private security expert until they were neck-deep in quicksand and needed one. And then they really, *really* wanted one.

"Can you hear anything good?"

Ryder jumped a mile high and whirled around in the same move. A petite woman in her early sixties with her ebony hair pulled back into a tight bun and no-nonsense, orthopedic granny shoes on her feet eyeballed Ryder with unblinking eyes.

Damn, she was so busted. Heat burned her cheeks. "George's secretary wasn't in and—"

"I'm Sarah Molina, Mr. Dylan's *executive assistant*. I apologize that my trip to the ladies' room was not timed for your convenience." She settled behind her desk and paused with her hands hovering above the keyboard. "Is there something I can help you with?"

Ryder bristled. She was eavesdropping, not stealing the crown jewels. "I'm here to see George. I have an appointment."

"Your name?"

"Ryder Falcon."

Sarah picked up the phone receiver and spoke quietly into it. "Mr. Dylan, there is a Ms. Falcon here to see you. She *says* she has an appointment." After half a minute of listening, she pursed her lips together in obvious displeasure and put the receiver down with an emphatic click. "You may go right in."

"Thanks." Ryder nodded, flicked her wrist, and turned the knob, pushing the door open. "Sorry to interrupt…"

The mystery man talking to the Dylan's Department Store CEO spun around to face her, and the rest of her spiel died on her tongue.

There were men she'd slept with and never thought

much about again. Then, there was a handful whose memory always put her in a good mood, like a cool beer on a warm night. Standing before her was the one man who'd bypassed the pleasant-buzz setting and had zoomed straight into the hardcore, make-your-panties-wet, two-shots-of-Tequilla-too-many danger zone.

An inch shy of six feet, Devin Harris had the body of a professional mixed martial arts fighter—complete with heavily inked skin—wrapped in a dark navy, pin-striped Brooks Brothers suit. He topped it off with short-clipped hair, model-worthy cheekbones, and a square jaw that would make Superman weep with jealousy. The combination of badass brawler and smooth corporate wolf sucked the smart-ass right out of her.

He was just her type, which was about as big of an indictment against him as there could be.

In a moment of epic bad judgment a few weeks ago, she'd ignored the quiet accountant types at the bar and had gone after the man she'd really wanted. Confident bordering on cocky. Sexy as hell. Too tempting for words. After their one night together and too many orgasms to count, she'd woken up wrapped in his arms, never wanting to leave even as she hated herself for falling back into old bad habits.

After Heath—after the hospital—she'd sworn never again.

So she'd snuck out of Mr. Temptation's bed, gone home, deleted his number from her phone, and blocked him. But that hadn't stopped her from thinking about him—and wondering foolishly if maybe he was different. If her guy radar wasn't completely for shit. But in the end she knew it was.

Recognition flickered in his latte-colored eyes, and her stomach did the loop-de-loop.

His mouth flattened into a straight line, and he crossed his arms. "George, tell me this is not the crack security professional you've been trying to sell me on."

Ryder's spine straightened like a whip snapping. The pompous prick.

"You forget yourself, Devin," George wheezed. "You work for me. I don't have to sell you on a damn thing."

• • •

Devin Harris bit back his scathing response because George was right, which shredded his ego like sandpaper on sliced Rye.

Ryder Falcon. Shit, with a name like that she should be in skin-tight red leather, fighting super villains in a comic book. Lord knew she was tough enough to make normal men quake in their pleated Dockers. He'd learned that for himself during their one hot night together when he'd licked his way down her toned abs and up her hard thighs.

It was a damn good thing he'd acquired an immunity to her particular brand of super-powered hotness in the three weeks since they'd hooked up. He barely noticed the way her tight body filled out the fitted, black suit that hugged her slim curves in all the right places. He'd already completely forgotten how she'd tasted of cinnamon, spice, and no-holds-barred sex so good his balls had practically sung the Hallelujah Chorus when he'd come the first time—and every other time that night. What he hadn't forgotten was that he'd woken up alone like a loser the next morning.

How many times had he called her cell only to be met by a deafening busy signal? His father may be right that he was just a stubborn ex-jock with a dented brain, but he'd finally gotten her message. The last thing he needed in his life was another woman who sent mixed signals—no matter how sexy she was. Been there. Done her. Never want to again.

"Ryder, I apologize for my right-hand man's rudeness. Let

me introduce you. Devin Harris is our general merchandise manager." George ambled around the desk, his over-indulged belly leading the way. "He blames himself for the troubles, which I've already told him is preposterous—unless, of course, he's the one syphoning off my cash." He chuckled at his own joke and held out his hand to Ryder. "Devin, this lovely lady is Ryder Falcon with Maltese Security."

She shook his hand, her jaw tightening when the CEO held on for a few beats too many. Irritation tightened Devin's spleen when he realized he'd actually counted how many seconds the handshake had lasted.

"Is there anyone who sticks out as a possible suspect?" she asked.

"All the signs point to Craig in accounting," Devin snarled. "I'm just choosing to ignore them because I want to sabotage the deal to take Dylan's Department Store global."

Even to himself, his sarcasm sounded like the spoiled, petulant teenager he used to be. Ryder didn't miss his snotty tone, either. She pivoted to face him. When he'd stripped her down to her see-through black bra and panties with her feet flat on the floor, she'd stood almost eye to eye with him. Today, in her heels, she added a good three inches to her height, putting her at just over six feet.

Looking up to a woman like Ryder would have some men on edge, but Devin relished the challenge she presented. Not that he wanted her under—or above—him again, but nothing got his blood pumping faster than someone telling him he couldn't do something.

And Ryder Falcon was a walking stop sign.

"I'm not questioning your abilities," she said in a tone that did just that. "I was simply starting my research. The more I know about the situation, the faster I'll be able to track down the embezzler and recover your lost funds."

George patted his stomach. "My thoughts exactly. That's

why I want you to come onboard and pose as Devin's personal assistant during the investigation. That will give you access to most of our people without raising too many eyebrows."

The wind rushed out of Devin's lungs as if he'd gotten a side kick to the chest. "What are you talking about?" His lungs ached with the effort of sputtering out the five words. "I can do this on my own."

Just looking at Ryder Falcon made him feel like he was on a roller coaster, and that annoyed the hell out of him. He'd spent most of his early life bouncing from good time to good time, living down to his father's constant and loudly expressed low expectations. Now, he appreciated the solid, the steady, the predictability of a five a.m. workout and a demanding job that left him elated and exhausted by eleven at night.

"It's perfectly logical to partner you two up. We need her expertise. She needs access, which you can give her. Everyone knows you're going through the books prior to the merger. And MulitCorp doesn't need to know anything about this little snafu before we finalize the merger next week. You and I both know they'll run like cockroaches when the lights come on if they even hear a rumor that our financials aren't what they're supposed to be. That gives you two a week to find the culprit and, hopefully, recover the stolen funds, before I have to give MultiCorp full access to our books prior to the final signatures."

Ryder's face had frozen into a neutral mask, but the way she twisted a strand of long, dark brown hair around a finger gave away her nervousness. "Sir, I can work much more efficiently and effectively on my own. There's really no need to involve Mr. Harris in this."

*Mr. Harris, was it?* That extra little bit of formality, considering the sweaty circumstances of their last meeting, woke up the natural antagonist in him. No way was she working a case alone, and she sure as hell wouldn't work it with anyone but him. "I don't know *Ms. Falcon*. If I remember correctly, we can work very well together."

If she could have slit him open with a look, his guts would have been spilled all over George's pin-neat desk.

The old man looked from one to the other, his eyes bloodshot but still keen as ever. "I didn't realize you two knew each other." No doubt he had picked up on the undercurrent and planned to exploit it to his best advantage. After all, the old man hadn't made Dylan's Department Store the must-shop-at experience for Harbor City's fashion elite by being slow-witted. "Isn't this perfect?"

Devin prowled across the office, every step closer making the color rise in her olive-complected cheeks, but she didn't give even an inch of ground. That fact excited him as much as the memory of her smooth skin under his tongue. "Don't worry, boss, we'll have this case solved before you know it."

"We?" Ryder's smooth alto tripped over the one syllable word.

"There's millions of dollars in cash and hundreds of millions in stocks on the line if the deal falls through." He stopped a few steps away from her, but close enough to peek into the deep V of her black linen blouse and notice the heated flush climbing up her cleavage. Looked like someone wasn't as unaffected by him as she pretended. "There's no way this happens without Dylan's representation every step of the way."

"Whatever you wish." She'd recovered enough to sprinkle just the right amount of insincerity in her tone, relaying her feelings on the matter without being openly rude. "You're the client."

Devin had been told, subtly and not so subtly, to fuck off too many times to count, but this was the first time that his only response was a twitch behind his zipper.

# Chapter Two

*"Strong women wear their pain like stilettos. No matter how much it hurts, all you see is the beauty of it."*

— *Harriet Morgan*

Chocolate was medically necessary if Ryder was going to make it through the next twenty-four hours. Well, that and some girl time in the form of gossip at Coffee Grounds with her best friends Drea and Sylvie. Every Thursday morning, they'd meet up at nine to swap gossip and inhale the carb-loaded goodness coming out of the in-house bakery.

Also, it was conveniently located three blocks from the third dimension of hell—also known as Devin Harris's office—so that meant she could sneak in for the regular chat and still report to her fake job on time.

A bell trilled as she pushed through the coffee shop's front doors. It only took a second to spot her best friends already lounging on the Burberry plaid loveseat facing the kitchen.

Those who lived and died by their daily dose of caffeine filled every other available seat, and more than a few of them were shooting dirty looks toward the duo on the couch.

"How did you manage to get such prime seats?" Ryder sat down in the red leather chair next to the loveseat.

"*Shhh*, doll baby," Drea whispered, her gaze fixed solidly over Ryder's left shoulder. "He's doing something to the dough that I wish he was doing to me."

The loveseat had become prime real estate ever since the world's hottest pastry chef started working at Coffee Grounds. The couch faced the glass wall dividing the front of the house from the kitchen, giving patrons a look into the inner workings of the coffee shop. Right now that meant watching the dark-haired delight in the white chef's jacket roll and knead the lightly floured dough in front of him. For a full minute, Drea didn't blink her eyes, which were done up in a thick cat's eye with white, shimmery powder that contrasted perfectly with her dark brown skin. As a makeup artist to Harbor City's elite fashionable set, Drea didn't do *au naturele*.

Ryder shook her head and giggled. "You are such a perv."

"Nah, I just know what I like and I'm not afraid to go get it." She slid her dark-eyed glance Ryder's way. "Unlike some people I know who seem to think they have some sort of dude curse."

Her chest tightened with a mix of irritation, embarrassment, and chagrin. She loved her best friends, but she'd made her decision of a commitment-free year to retrain her guy-dar so she'd stop falling for the same brand of shithead as she had in the past and she was sticking to it.

"Don't you start in, too, Drea." She took a sip of the double mocha latte already waiting for her on the table. Nothing settled her nerves as much as knowing she had good friends who knew her well enough to get her emergency order without even asking. "Sylvie is already riding me about my year of no relationships. I've been practicing serial monogamy with one loser after another since I was eighteen. You can't deny I'm an asshole magnet. Anyway, I can't go through what happened with Heath again."

Anxiety formed a lump in her throat. Just the idea of falling hard for the wrong guy again had her stomach doing the rhumba. Had she gone overboard? Maybe. But she wasn't about to admit it.

Sylvie leaned forward and snagged a chocolate crumpet. "That's the dumbest thing I've ever heard of." Her smile softened her words. "We've all had our hearts broken by jerks, and Heath was in a class of his own, but that was more than a year ago. Don't you think it's time to get back out there?"

"You say that like I'm not dating. I am." Okay, that might be a stretch. It was more like an experiment in keeping it all physical without any of the emotional stuff.

"Just not the same guy twice. Or anyone you're really interested in." Sylvie retorted.

"Do I need to go down the ex hall of shame again? It's a long fucking list, capped off by Heath, the guy who lied about everything and tried to beat the shit out of me when I confronted him about it."

Drea said, "The chances of you getting duped by a catfish scheme twice in one lifetime by an abusive dickwad are pretty fucking low." She dragged her focus away from the pastry chef. "Heath, or whatever the hell his name really is, lied to you online, pretended to be someone he wasn't, and went so far as to share fake pics of his dog with his dying mom to convince you he was legit. It's how scum like him operates. They build trust. You did your due diligence—"

"And yet I still ended up in the emergency room with a broken wrist and a black eye." Ryder squirmed in her seat, wishing more than anything she could take out her own shortcomings on a kick bag. After she'd gotten the cast off her wrist, she'd returned to Paulie's Gym and rediscovered herself. Each punch and every kick made her stronger, safer, and more in control. That's where she'd come up with her one-date-only policy. It was like a hard reboot of her system that she hoped would reset her sense of attraction.

Sylvie squeezed her hand. "You can't blame yourself for someone else's actions. Heath is to blame. Not you. You didn't do anything wrong. All you're doing now is shutting yourself off to life's possibilities."

"I have my reasons." Grabbing hold of her mile-wide stubborn streak like a life preserver on open waters, she forced her fidgeting body to still. "No one else in the world but you two knows exactly what they are, and I'd like to keep it that way."

Drea's full lips settled into a thin line. "What I know is that you're using that fucked up situation with that asshole to tread water. Life is always moving forward, and you have to move with it. Holding onto all that dead weight does nothing for you but give you bags under your eyes that my makeup brush can't hide."

"I thought there was nothing you couldn't fix."

"Don't try to butter me up, doll baby. I am un-butter-up-able." Drea sipped her chai tea. "But you're right. I'm damn good."

Ryder couldn't stop the laugh bubbling up inside as she glanced down at her watch. "Shit, I'm going to have to blaze soon."

"Big case?" Sylvie asked.

"Sort of." Ryder popped a chocolate pastry bite into her mouth, and pleasure rippled from her tongue throughout her body. Damn, that chef was good to look at *and* made the most divine goodies. She might just throw down with Drea for him. "I'm going undercover as a personal assistant for a few days."

"And you thought assistants dressed like that chick from

*The Matrix*?" Sylvie asked.

Ryder smoothed her hand against her black pencil skirt and made sure all the buttons on her black button down were fastened. "She wasn't wearing a skirt."

Sylvie shook her head. "Ryder."

"Come on. Besides, Mom got me this skirt."

"For a funeral, no doubt." Drea bumped fists with Sylvie. "Doll baby, there is nothing wrong with adding a little color to your all-black wardrobe. Come on, get crazy."

"No way. The last time I let you talk me into breaking out of my comfort zone, I ended up in bed with my new client."

Both women's jaws hit the floor.

Heat ate its way north from her chest. "You remember… The guy from the club. A few weeks ago. Muscles? Tattoos? Ass worth crying over? Totally my type and, therefore, exactly the kind of guy I should stay the hell away from?" She looked from one shocked face to the other. "Come on, I know I told you about him." The one who'd tempted her beyond all reason to come back for seconds and thirds and fourths.

Sylvie tossed a crumpled up napkin at her. "The question is how did you wait this long to tell us he's your new client?"

"Playing a little boss and secretary, eh?" Drea asked. "Who's the perv now?"

An image of stripping down to her heels while Devin sat behind his desk flashed in her mind, and her whole body began to tingle. "Don't even put that image in my head. I'm not falling off the wagon again."

Always ready for any matchmaking opportunity, Sylvie's green eyes lit up. "Is he the guy you wouldn't call back?"

She locked her gaze on the last drops of mocha latte in her cup. "That's the one."

"Remind me again why you ended up blocking him from your phone?"

"Like I said, he's just my type—my old type." She reached

for her purse. The girls were circling, and she knew better than to stick around when they decided it was time to offer some older sister advice. She loved them, but sometimes being the youngest in the group sucked big hairy goat balls.

"So the hot, muscled, tattooed guy with a great job who's fabulous in bed and more than a little bit interested in you isn't your type?" Drea asked. "And then, after you blocked him, you spent the next week at Paulie's Gym punching things. That had nothing to do with this guy at all?"

Ryder nodded and stood, ready to bolt. "Exactly."

Sylvie and Drea exchanged a she's-full-of-shit glance, but Ryder ignored it. It didn't matter. She wasn't about to let personal feelings fuck up this case. From here on out, she was all business.

• • •

Devin rubbed the back of his neck and pushed his way to the rear of elevator at Dylan's Department Store. As soon as the doors closed, the baby in the stroller lost his mind. The kid's screams jabbed through Devin's eardrums and marched down his spine like an army of ants wearing razor-sharp cleats. The woman, whom he assumed was the mom, had the frazzled, embarrassed, and at-the-end-of-her-rope look of someone who'd been on the receiving end of a baby's anger and stranger's disapproval for most of the day.

It reminded him of the last walk he'd taken with his little brother, James, outside of the long-term care facility. A police cruiser came roaring by with the lights flashing and siren blaring. James had clapped his hands over his ears and howled in fear before crumpling to the ground. Strangers had given them wide berth as they hustled past on the sidewalk. No one tried to help. Not like they could. Devin had made sure of that years ago.

The mother picked up the fussy baby and hugged him close, cooing ineffectually in his ear.

"Sorry." She glanced back over her shoulder at the others in the elevator before quickly turning to face front again. "He's teething."

While the elevator inched toward the lobby floor, the other riders ignored her remark and continued to aim dirty looks at the back of her head. She bounced the kid up and down, jiggling him in a failed attempt to calm him, but the red-faced creature didn't give a shit about the censure. He just kept screaming.

Devin scrunched up his face and made fish lips at the kid. The yelling continued, but the volume dropped a few decibels. He pulled his Stefano Ricci micro-neat silk tie away from his shirt, stuck his fingertips into the pointy end, and curled it toward himself before making faces at it as if the light blue Italian tie was a puppet. The screaming silenced, but the kid's mouth stayed poised to emit a deafening racket at any moment.

He eyed Devin warily.

Smart kid.

Time to break out the big guns. He let go of his tie and covered his face with his hands, waited a beat, then opened them up. The baby giggled at the peek-a-boo game, showing off two tiny front teeth in an otherwise gummy smile. Devin disappeared again behind his hands just as a *ping* sounded, announcing the elevator had arrived at the lobby level.

The doors slid open in sync with Devin's hands, revealing a smiling baby being carried out into the flood of people at the elevator banks. Dead in the center of the crowd stood Ryder Falcon, looking at him like he'd lost his ever-loving mind.

He immediately dropped his hands and shoved them deep into his pockets.

"You coming out?" Ryder asked, a grin tugging the corners of her mouth.

*Smooth move, Harris. You're such a stud.* "No. I was heading down to meet you in the lobby."

She strode into the elevator, looking every inch like she owned the building, and met his gaze with her unwavering eyes. "Well, here I am."

"Here you are." He shut his trap before he blew her away with any more of his oh-so-amazing verbal skills.

The influx of people marching onto the elevator put that awkward conversation out of its misery, which was a blessing. Until, that is, the crowd pushed Ryder farther and farther back so that she stood directly in front of him with only a bare minimum of space between their bodies. From that small distance, even a saint would have imagined how good her butt looked encased in a black pencil skirt.

They rode up to the executive level in wary silence. By the time they arrived, they were the only ones left in the elevator, and the taunting cinnamon scent of her perfume was seriously testing his patience. This attraction was just going to slow him down in this investigation, but damn if standing this close to her didn't make taking it slow seem appealing. He shook himself. What had happened between them a few weeks ago didn't matter. All that mattered was finding the embezzler and getting the books fixed before they had to open them to MultiCorp.

George might have foisted Ryder on him, but that didn't mean Devin wouldn't control every step of this investigation. He knew too well from personal experience that ceding control led only to very bad things.

They stepped out onto the fifteenth floor. The first ten floors of Dylan's Department Store's flagship store were for shopping. Floors eleven through fourteen were administration offices. The top floor was reserved for Dylan's Department Store's executives. It had been his home for the past ten years, and he'd do whatever it took to safeguard the store's success.

He wouldn't fail at this, too.

Jane Anndra sat at her post at the main reception desk opposite the elevator. A veteran at Dylan's Department Store, she knew everything and everyone. Introducing Ryder would be the fastest way to get this farce George had cooked up to the boiling point.

"So what's on the agenda today, sir?" Ryder smiled at him, the picture of an eager new employee, and pulled a notepad and pen out of her oversize ebony Calvin Klein tote bag that matched her all-black ensemble.

"Let's start with introductions. Jane, this is Ryder Falcon. She's my new personal assistant."

The receptionist was too much of a pro to show an overt reaction to his announcement, but he swore her eyebrow moved up a fraction of an inch. "And what exactly does that mean?"

He shrugged. "Your guess is as good as mine. George insisted."

"I'm sure he did." Jane gave Ryder an up and down glance. "Speaking of Mr. Dylan, he is at a bit of a loss today. Sarah called in sick." Jane narrowed her eyes at Ryder and *tutt*ed. "I'm assuming you're going to need access to the employee improvement fund?"

The fund was a catchall for everything from new baby presents to wedding gifts, to you-did-a-great-job rewards. Since Ryder wasn't pregnant, wasn't married, and had just started here, none of it applied to her.

"For what?" he asked.

Jane used her pen as a pointer, leveling it at Ryder. "Her clothes."

"What's wrong with my clothes?" Ryder sputtered as she smoothed her hands down her discount black skirt from several seasons ago.

"Your clothes are perfectly suitable, my dear." Tactful but firm, Jane continued. "But they're not really what one would expect on the fifteenth floor."

The glimmer of an idea flickered in Devin's periphery vision. George said he didn't have any choice in working with Maltese Security, but that didn't mean another agent couldn't stand in as his assistant. Judging by the tension emanating from Ryder's tight body, she hated the idea of a mandated makeover, hopefully enough to ask to be reassigned.

"Excellent idea, Jane." He pressed the elevator's down button. "If you need me, we'll be in the luxury women's department of the fifth floor."

• • •

Twenty minutes and a pile of frighteningly bright dresses later, Ryder was ready to pull her Beretta in the middle of the poshest private shopping area in all of Harbor City. Sylvie and Drea would be in heaven at the idea of playing Barbie as part of an all-expenses-paid makeover, but Ryder dug in her heels and stared down the diminutive woman holding a fuchsia, cap sleeve dress from ESCADA. Used to her all-black wardrobe, the color blinded her, but not enough that she failed to notice the four-digit price tag. Kailer might be the stylist to all of the most famous shoppers at Dylan's Department Store, but the woman was certifiable if she thought Ryder would be caught dead in that color.

"I don't think so." Just because she was pretending to be Devin's assistant didn't mean she lost all of her own power. She'd stood up to worse and won.

Not for the first time in the twenty minutes they'd been together in the roped-off private shopping area, Kailer huffed hard enough to send her thick auburn bangs fluttering upward. The stylist glanced over her shoulder at Devin, who was talking on the phone as he paced through the empty showroom. This area was open by appointment only—unless you were the number two at Dylan's Department Store, and then it seemed you could torture people in there any time you wanted.

Not finding help from her distracted superior, Kailer turned back to Ryder and held up a cherry red dress. "Trust me, I'm a stylist. I dress people for a living. This one would be lovely with your skin tone. It's a Burberry London, drape-front, mulberry silk dress. The design detail in the front helps to add interest. You'll look perfect."

Ryder crossed her arms. She wouldn't be manipulated by anyone again. "I don't want a new dress."

Kailer's bright blue eyes took on the weary hue of a woman for whom a three-martini lunch had become a foregone conclusion. "But Mr. Harris—"

"Can kiss my ass."

A large shadow appeared, eliciting a delicious shiver up Ryder's spine.

Devin cleared his throat. "Kailer, can you excuse us for a moment?"

"Of course." The stylist hightailed it out of the roped-off, private shopping area faster than expected, considering her short legs.

"This is ridiculous." Ryder rounded on him, hands on her hips and ready for a fight. "Being your Eliza Doolittle is not part of the job."

He fingered the red silk dress hanging on the garment rack. "It is if you want to fit in and get people to answer your questions."

Of all the stupid things. How superficial were these people? "I don't—"

"Look, I'm the general merchandise manager for Dylan's Department Store, the most luxurious store for the fashion-conscious in the country. That means I head a team of fashion buyers, merchandisers, and senior executives focused only on finding the most on-trend and profitable clothing and accessories to sell to our customers. I can't have my assistant looking like the runway from two years ago. Fashion is these people's passion and my bread and butter."

Damn, she hated it when he made sense. But unfortunately, he did.

"I still don't like it." She crossed her arms.

"Lucky for you, fashion doesn't require you to actually like it." He stormed off to the cream leather chairs opposite the dressing rooms. "Kailer, she's all yours."

Thirty minutes and sixteen dress arguments later, the stylist's face had taken on the determined devotional sheen of a high-priestess of fashion intent on making Ryder a convert.

"I think I found the one!" Kailer removed a royal blue dress from a stuffed garment rack near the three-way mirror. "It's a matte jersey from the St. John Collection. It will move with you and be very comfortable. The asymmetrical collar gives it a touch of drama. What do you think?"

Ryder held it up and looked in the mirror. Of all the choices so far, it came the closest, but the color was so not black.

"Right dress." Devin got up from the couch where he'd been glued to his phone and strolled over to the garment rack. He pulled out the same dress in darkest ebony. "Wrong color."

Ryder traded the blue for the black, glanced down at the price tag. One dress or groceries for the foreseeable future? An easy choice. "I can't."

"You can." Devin hung the blue dress on the rack. "Or we'll be down here all day. Consider it a gift."

God, it was soft—she held it against her frame—and so pretty. "It's too expensive."

"It's yours. Kailer, wrap it up and include the others in black as well." He turned toward the elevator. "Come on, Ryder, we have work to do."

# Chapter Three

*"Fashion is like a revolving door. Sometimes you get stuck in it."*

— *Milana May*

Storm clouds had gathered outside Devin's windows when Ryder barreled into his office, her hair a wild, wavy mane around her shoulders. As always, she was dressed in head-to-toe black, this time the Armani, sleeveless sheath dress from the spring collection that showed off her toned arms and her muscled calves.

He shook his head. Fifteen years ago, all he would have noticed was her firm ass, not the clothes, and for sure not what they were called or when they'd debuted. Of course, back then he would have been too hung over at nine in the morning to even crack his eyes open.

All five-foot-ten-inches of blue-ball-inducing sexiness of her pulled to a stop in front of his desk.

For the past two days, she'd all but ignored him as she went through page after page of the store's financials. He'd had a desk installed for her in the corner of his office so she could do her job without worrying about prying eyes. It had seemed like a good idea at the time. Talk about theory versus reality. It had turned his office into a level of hell even Dante hadn't considered.

Seeing Ryder twist her long hair around one finger only reminded him of how smooth the dark strands had felt on his stomach as she'd kissed her way south during their one night together. And then there was the way she mumbled to herself as she ran numbers in a low voice that vibrated down to his balls. The result being that he hadn't sported this much useless wood since he'd been a teenager.

"We've got a problem." Ryder held a manila folder in her hand. "There's a lot more than just a million dollars gone."

Visions of her spread out beneath him on his bed fled in a heartbeat. His gut bounced against the floor. Shit, he needed to pull it together. "What are you talking about?"

"Four point seven million."

White noise buzzed in his ears as he tried to process the bomb she'd just tossed into his lap. "That's impossible."

"Not really." She paced in front of his desk. "Embezzlers don't act like bank robbers—at least, not the good ones. They don't run in, stuff as much cash in a bag as they can, and then split. They're like car salesmen. They want to take some money from you this year and the next and the year after that. The smart embezzlers are in it for the long haul. I've spent the past few days going through your books with a fine-tooth comb. What I noticed was that one particular account had consistent growth. The more I looked, the more it looked off. So I dug into the records and discovered vendor invoices from businesses that never existed."

"How do you know they don't exist?" Anxiety pulled

every muscle in his body tight. If this was true, the MultiCorp deal could collapse. Everything he'd worked to make happen for the last three years would be gone. The international market would be closed to Dylan's for the foreseeable future.

"I'm an investigator. It's what I do." She stopped in front of his desk with her hands planted on her hips. "There's more. The bogus invoices go back fifteen years. That equates to more than three-hundred-thousand dollars a year."

Anger ripped through him, leaving him raw and hurting from the inside out. He turned on the messenger, ready to blast her out into the thunderstorm brewing outside his window.

"And you were able to figure all this out in what, forty-two hours, when we have some of the best accounting staff in the industry and they've never noticed a thing?"

She shrugged, but stood her ground. "They weren't looking for someone doing them wrong. They were double checking that every check request came with an invoice and that the amounts matched. The culprit is familiar enough with Dylan's inner workings to be able to produce the verification needed and controlled enough to keep from getting greedy."

"You call 4.7 million not greedy?"

"Considering the damage he could have done? Yeah."

"He?" Dread curled up in his stomach like a lead cat.

"Yep, all of the check requests have the same signature."

"Whose?" Just getting out the single word hurt.

"The one person that no one would ever question."

In a heartbeat, the room went from climate controlled to Florida in August. "That's ridiculous."

She flipped open the manila envelope lying in front of him. His lungs closed, leaving him stock-still in his chair and hearing only the blood rushing in his ears.

"Go on. Look." She tapped the paper.

He hated her at that moment because he didn't need to

look to know whose signature would be slashed across the papers. "I'm sure there's an explanation."

"Let's go find out what it is."

The challenge hung in the air between them, a red flag in the bull fighting arena.

"George is my mentor, my boss, and the man who gave me a chance when even my own father had given up on me. That's not the kind of man who steals from his own company."

Her jaw clenched and she looked over his left shoulder as rain pelted the windows. "People cheat and lie about who they really are all the time."

It didn't make sense.

It couldn't make sense.

"He's got more money than God and he controls eighty percent of Dylan's Department Store stock. His name is on the damn building for Christ's sake. Why would he even need to pull a stunt like this?"

"Because as it stands now, the store only has another five years before the vultures start circling."

He slammed his palms on the desk and shot out of his chair. The need to protect his mentor's reputation beat a fast rhythm through his veins. "Now you're just talking crazy."

"No. I've studied the books. You need this merger."

"Of course we do, it'll open up the international market to our brand."

"And you need the cash infusion or trouble is imminent."

"Trouble?"

"Yeah, the kind that usually involves contract renegotiations at best and bankruptcy judges at worst."

"That's crap. You're wrong about George."

"Maybe." She crossed her arms and glared down at him from her standing position. "But I'm not wrong about these numbers or the signatures. They aren't forgeries."

"How do you know that?"

"Detailed comparison under a microscope. There's no sign of a forger's tremor, unevenness in pen pressure, or patching."

"Patching?"

"When someone forges something, often they'll touch up a faulty stroke or writing feature, like the extra flair on the *G* in George's signature."

"Let's go." He circled his desk and marched to the door, yanking it open with enough force to startle his secretary on the other side.

"Where are we going?" A wary edge hardened Ryder's alto voice.

He didn't care. This wasn't just some case to him. This was his life. "To the old man's office."

• • •

A frazzled woman in her mid-forties sat at Sarah Molina's desk outside George's office. Powered by righteous indignation, Devin didn't even pause to ask for entry before barreling through the double doors leading to his boss's inner sanctum.

"I'll do the talking," he snarled over his shoulder to Ryder.

The old man sat behind his desk, the phone receiver pressed to his ear.

He glared at Devin and Ryder. "Yes, of course, I really appreciate this, Louis. Devin and his personal assistant will be taking the company jet out first thing in the morning. Dylan's Department Store is thrilled to finally have a presence at Andol Fashion Week. And as for that other thing, I cannot thank you enough."

The Andol Republic was an island nation off the cost of Chile. Small but influential in the world of fashion, in the same way as Cannes to the world of film.

Bristling with energy that begged for an outlet, Devin

forced himself to be still. He'd fought too fucking hard to put the act-first, reason-second mentality behind him to give in now. Next to him, he could practically feel Ryder humming with excitement like a vibrating bed in a cheap motel. To her this was just a case and she thought she'd nailed it. Behind them the secretary hovered in the doorway, too nervous or scared to come in any farther.

George hung up the phone. "This had better be damn good for you to barge in here when I'm on the phone with The Andol Republic's cultural minister."

Lightning lit the sky behind him.

"I'm sorry, sir." A thunderclap drowned out the rest of the soft-spoken secretary's apology.

"It's not your fault, Suzie. By the looks of him, it would have taken a dozen navy SEALs to keep him out." He jerked his chin toward the door. "Why don't you take an early lunch?"

"But Mrs. Molina's notes said not to take a lunch until you did, and even then to eat it quickly in the break room."

"Well, Mrs. Molina is out sick, so I guess that means I'm in charge, and I'm giving you an early lunch. Why don't you go check out the new cafe that just opened up next to housewares on the sixth floor? I imagine the tomato basil soup would really hit the spot on a day like today."

Another lightning bolt exploded in the distance. Devin counted while the secretary backed out of the room. One. Two. *Boom!* The thunder shook the plate glass window. He'd have to call and check in on James soon. The lightning storms that used to fascinate his little brother now frightened him. Too often the nurses found him hiding under his bed during storms like this.

The door clicked shut, bringing Devin back to the here and now. The red flush in the old man's cheeks didn't make an impact—he'd learned a long time ago that George was all bluster and no bang.

He'd hustled into the CEO's corner office without pausing to figure out what in the hell he was going to say. It wasn't like he could come out and tell his mentor that the obviously-off-her-rocker investigator thought George had embezzled from his own company. Devin rubbed his palm against his close-cropped hair and opened his mouth.

Ryder stepped forward. "Can you explain why your signature ended up on all these false reimbursement requests?" She handed the manila folder to George.

The old man quirked an eyebrow but accepted the folder.

*What the hell?* Devin whipped his head around so fast it almost rolled off his neck. He'd told her to let him do the talking. *This was his show, dammit.* "I told her the whole idea is ridiculous."

George held up his palm for silence as he ran his finger down the center of each page. After a few minutes, he sighed and softly closed the folder. "It looks to me as though my faith in Maltese Security is not unfounded. It seems you've found our embezzler."

The shock of his statement almost snapped Devin's head back.

"My arthritis has made signing documents tedious, and I had a signature stamp made up years ago that I keep locked in my desk. Only two people have the key. Myself and my executive assistant, Sarah Molina." George picked up a single sheet of paper from his desk and handed it to Ryder. "You need to see this. I found this in my inter-company mail this morning. It was deposited two days ago, but got lost in the mailroom. I was going to give it to you after my call with The Andol Republic's cultural minister. You'll understand why as soon as you read it. Why don't you do that out loud?"

She glanced down. Her brown eyes rounded and her chin jerked up.

George slumped back in his chair and pinched the bridge

of his nose. "Go on. Get it over with."

"DEAR GEORGE. THIRTY YEARS AGO, I CHOSE YOU OVER MY HOME AND MY FAMILY. I LEARNED TOO LATE WHAT A MISTAKE I'D MADE, BUT DON'T WORRY. I'M DONE WITH YOU AND WITH DYLAN'S DEPARTMENT STORE. I KNOW THIS BUSINESS BETTER THAN YOU EVER COULD, BUT YOU NEVER SAW THAT. TO YOU I WAS JUST AN EXECUTIVE ASSISTANT ON A GOOD DAY AND A LACKEY ON A BAD ONE. BUT DON'T WORRY, I MADE SURE TO BUILD MY OWN GOLDEN PARACHUTE. SARAH MOLINA."

Ice water rushed through Devin's veins and he forgot to breathe for a second, but then the pieces clicked into place. George's executive secretary had called in sick for the first time in five years the day after Ryder joined the investigation. Sarah had access to almost everything George did. If anyone could game the system, it would be the woman who'd been the power behind the throne for thirty years. "Sarah."

"Yes," George grumbled. "She always did have to have the last word."

Ryder recovered from her shock first. "We know the who, now we just have to find her."

"I already know where she is." George grabbed a sheet of paper decorated with an Internet travel booking site's logo. "Sarah didn't bother to try to cover her tracks. She's in The Andol Republic."

"So we'll contact the authorities, present the evidence, and have her extradited," Ryder said.

Devin's left eye twitched and a jarring pain crackled through his brain. He had about an hour before the mother of all stress migraines tried its best to lay him flat.

"The Andol Republic does not have an extradition agreement with the United States," George said.

Ryder stared at the rain lashing the windows as the dark gray clouds tumbled across the sky. "Well, we can't go down there and kidnap her."

"True, but my friend, the cultural minister, has agreed to bless our removing Sarah from Andol soil—after the fact." George sat forward and propped his elbows on his desk. "For political reasons, he cannot support our efforts publicly beforehand. It seems her family is well connected down there in the bent-nose kind of way."

The old man had lost it. The pressure of the merger combined with the store's financial troubles had finally made him crack.

"So are you suggesting we go down there guns blazing, grab her, and bring her back?" Devin spoke slowly, as though he were chatting with someone who'd gone off their meds.

"Not exactly. The Andol Fashion Week is kicking off tomorrow." George opened a drawer and removed two folders, which he handed to Ryder and Devin. "You'll travel down as Dylan's Department Store's official representation, attend a few shows from the hottest South American designers, and then return home—with an extra undocumented passenger. Once you're home, we'll turn Sarah over to the authorities, and with any luck, recover the money she stole."

Devin scoffed. "You make it sound so simple."

"Come on now, you should know better than most… Life so rarely is."

# Chapter Four

*"Whoever said that money can't buy happiness, simply didn't know where to go shopping."*

— *Bo Derek*

The Dylan Corporation hadn't scrimped when it came to outfitting the corporate jet. There were cream-colored leather seats as soft as a baby's butt, hand-cut crystal decanters secured behind glass cabinet doors, and a discrete attendant who, once they reached cruising altitude, pointed out the call button and disappeared into the cockpit for the remainder of the flight.

Ryder should have been basking in the luxury. Instead, she was as twitchy as a dog rescued from a puppy mill. She hated flying.

Hated. It.

The innate vulnerability of sailing through the clouds in a metal tube always put her on edge. Usually, the key to surviving a flight was a slight buzz and deep breaths, but not today. First off, Tony would kill her if she shotgunned a beer in front of a client. And, more important, every time she inhaled, the citrusy scent that had clung to a certain man's bed sheets taunted her.

The main reason for the tension tightening her thighs sat less than four feet away at a built-in table. Devin had ditched his suit jacket and rolled up the sleeves of his baby blue dress shirt, revealing the bright green dragon that curled up his forearm as one part of an intricate full sleeve tattoo. As he typed on his laptop, his muscles undulated, giving the dragon the illusion of movement. He'd also loosened his tie and unbuttoned his shirt collar, allowing a glimpse of the abstract design covering his hard pecs.

If she hadn't run a background check on Devin, Ryder would have sworn he'd grown up, like her, in the working class neighborhoods of Waterberg, far from the ritzy urban enclaves of Harbor City. Talk about being dead wrong. Even if she had a hundred dollars for every pasta noodle she'd eaten in her life, she wouldn't put a dent in his trust fund.

Devin cleared his throat, never pausing his pounding on the keyboard or bothering to look her way. "You're staring."

Yeah, so damn hard her eyeballs were about to fall out. Blinking rapidly, she straightened in the bucket seat and picked an invisible piece of lint from her black chiffon tank top while running through a mental list of shitty ex-boyfriends to remind herself of why she needed to stop ogling her client. No matter how hot he was.

"I was wondering how a white-bread, private-school-attending, eating-Sunday-brunch-at-the-club dude like you ended up with a healthy start to a tattoo bodysuit." There. That should put him on the defensive.

His fingers paused on the keyboard. "Ten years as a carny." The *clickity clack* revved back up to full speed.

Score one for the rich kid. "Tilt-a-Whirl?"

The *clack*ing ceased. He leaned back in his seat and arched his neck from side to side in a move natural to every jock she'd ever dated. Next, he rolled his shoulders under the perfectly-tailored shirt and leveled a heated gaze at her. Appraising and full of dark promise, the look made her clothes too tight to contain her suddenly aching boobs, and her lungs too small to hold the proper amount of oxygen.

"Kissing booth." He turned his attention back to his laptop.

Years ago, Ryder's mother had warned her never to poke a bear with a stick. While she'd always remembered her mother's advice, she hadn't taken it then and she wasn't going to now.

Big, grumpy bears didn't scare her. She liked hearing them growl.

Ryder *tsk-tsk*ed. "Funny, I figured you for a big draw at the dunk tank."

His fingers froze.

A shiver of anticipation danced down her spine. Picking a fight with a client might not be the smartest move, but it was so much better than sprinting across the aisle and jumping his bones at five thousand feet. The butterflies in her stomach disagreed, but what did they know about anything?

"Here's the brief on Sarah Molina." He clicked a button on his laptop, and her tablet *ping*ed in her black fake-ostrich-skin tote. "That should entertain you for a while."

• • •

Trapped in midair, halfway into the nine-hour flight, Devin acted out his own version of Jack typing in the old Steven King movie, *The Shining*. But he was punching random letters on the keyboard to keep the horny away instead of the crazy.

The looney in this case sat curled up in the seat across the aisle, her bare feet tucked under her pert ass. Dragging his gaze back to the mumbo-jumbo on the screen, he went back to pummeling the keyboard.

Ryder wasn't the first woman who had hightailed it the other way from him without any prior hint of dissatisfaction. Hell, a man couldn't get to twenty-eight without at least one raging-bad breakup, but she was the first who'd sneaked out at dawn while he was drooling on his pillow.

He'd woken up that morning to an empty bed. The air had still been thick with the smell of sex, and his balls had been as heavy as fifty-pound barbells. She'd ignored a week's worth of follow-up texts and calls. That kind of rejection stuck in a man's craw—especially when he couldn't stop thinking about the woman who'd run away.

Ryder crossed the aisle and slid into the bench seat on the opposite side of the table. Wispy hints of her heady cinnamon perfume reached out to him and sent his thoughts back to that night in his bed—although judging by the tightness behind his zipper some parts of his anatomy had never left the rumpled sheets.

She tapped her tablet screen and brought up the first page of Sarah Molina's employment record. "So, Sarah has been Dylan's executive assistant for thirty years?"

"Yep, she climbed the corporate ladder with him. Rumor is she had to yank him up a few rungs, but she did it." Grateful for the safe distraction from where his thoughts kept traveling, he relaxed back against the booth.

"His father founded the company. Why wouldn't he float up that ladder?"

"George had some wild days when he was younger. He and my dad refer to them as the lost years."

Devin had more than a few of those lost years himself, documented in bright ink across his body. He hadn't gotten them as a carney as he'd told her, but training as a mixed martial arts fighter had seemed like a circus.

"Your dad and George are old buddies, huh?" She tilted her head. "Never hurts to have connections."

She didn't come right out and say "spoiled rich kid," but he got the drift loud and clear. Of course, she didn't understand that his father had demanded a hefty price for the privilege of being born with the last name Harris and the bank account that came with it. Devin had rebelled by being just the kind of reckless idiot his father had always told him he was. His brother, a certifiable genius, had stayed on the straight and narrow, but had still suffered the Harris family curse…in a way far worse than just dealing with daddy's disapproval.

"Depends on the connection." Refusing to go any farther along that dangerous path, he scrolled down his notes on the laptop. "Sarah used her company computer and email address to book her tickets to The Andol Republic."

Ryder glanced up at the ceiling and sucked on her bottom lip, obviously mulling the facts. "She is either dumb as a box of rocks, wants to get caught, or doesn't care that we know she's the embezzler. Which do you think we're dealing with?"

"She's not dumb." He shook his head. Iron-willed. Mean as a wet cat. Deviously determined. Oh, yeah, those pretty much summed up the executive assistant who'd spent three decades by George's side. "I think she's pissed off."

"Why?"

"George hired a second executive assistant eons ago, about the time when the money started going missing. Sarah didn't take it well. There was a big dust-up, but George wouldn't relent. Then about a month ago, he hired another young assistant. You remember Suzie, the frazzled receptionist from yesterday?" When he paused, Ryder shot him a pointed stare that practically screamed, "*Get on with it.*" "Sarah is territorial and doesn't want anyone messing with her turf."

"And her turf was George Dylan."

He nodded.

"So had they ever mixed business with pleasure?"

"No idea. And I don't want to know." He shook off the image with a grimace. There were some people he never wanted to imagine buck naked and doing the nasty. George was at the top of that list. "What may or may not have happened between them doesn't concern us. We need to get to Andol, find Sarah, and get the money back."

"What about contacting the local police?"

Heat seared his lungs and spread through his shoulders, down his arms, and out his fingers. "Not gonna happen. If word leaks about this snafu, I can kiss the merger good-bye—and probably my job, too."

"You think George would fire you?"

"He gave me a chance when no one else in the world would, and he'd still fight for me today, but the Dylan Corporation board is a whole other barracuda. Someone's going to have to take the fall. It's not going to be the guy with his name on the building."

She clucked her tongue against the back of her teeth, drawing his attention to her glossy pink lips. "Your brief mentions Sarah's originally from The Andol Republic."

Glancing out the window to the patchwork green of South America below, he centered his focus back where it should be: catching Sarah. His career was riding on the merger deal. If this blew sky high, he might as well stay in The Andol Republic himself and become a beach bum.

"Most of her family is on the island. She had some kind of fight with them and left when she was young—shortly after George visited when his first marriage busted up. Sarah never went back to visit home, but she'd swore to George that she'd go back someday."

"Looks like that day came."

"But not for long." He poured a finger of whiskey into a crystal tumbler, then poured a second. Leaning forward, he took a whiff. The strong scent of bourbon burned along his nostrils followed by the hint of orange peel and gingersnaps. He pushed one of the glasses across the table to Ryder. "It's Four Roses Single Barrel."

She wrapped her fingers around the glass and lifted it to her lips. Devin reached out, halting the tumbler inches from its intended target.

"This isn't for shooting. It's for sipping. It comes from specially aged bourbon barrels and has a high rye content that creates a spicy, yet fruity, flavor." He released her glass and held his own aloft, touching the rims together. "To all of the things we have and all we still want—and to truces."

A Mona Lisa smile curved her lips as she stared at the amber liquid. "To truces." Despite his orders, the stubborn woman shot back half the glass.

They worked in companionable silence until Ryder started grumbling under her breath. "Tell me again why I can't go online? I thought every private jet had wifi."

She drummed her fingers on the tabletop. Irritation colored her cheeks as she twisted a long strand of dark brown hair around a finger. The move was the last thing he should be noticing right now, but damned if he could stop staring.

Pulling himself back from the brink before his cock realized where his thoughts were going, Devin shot back the last of his bourbon. "You ride a lot of private jets?"

"No, but my butt's in coach every few months and even the discount airliners offer in-flight Internet."

"You'll have to ask George why there's no wifi."

She rolled her eyes, her expression clearly telling him to fuck off. "I'll add it to the list."

The plane bobbled in the air, sending the empty crystal tumblers onto their sides. They rolled across the inlaid table and bounced back from the wall a second before the captain's voice sounded over the intercom. "Sir, we're approaching a patch of weather. I'm going to do my best to keep things smooth, but I need you to please buckle up."

Devin grabbed the glasses and put them in the designated container, then slid across the bench seat so he could get to the seats with the safety belts. But Ryder didn't move. Her finger worked double time twirling her hair while her other hand held onto the table edge with a death grip. The sight kicked him somewhere soft and resurrected the protective instincts he thought had died after the accident that almost killed his brother.

"Come on." Devin stood and held out his hand. "Let's get you buckled in."

Her gaze snapped up, scared but defiant. "I'm fine right here."

As if the fates were mocking her, the plane did a little dip that nearly jostled him off his feet. He threw out his hands to maintain his balance.

She pinched her lips together tight enough that a white line zipped around the edges. He grasped her wrist and tugged, coaxing her out of her comfort zone. Like the skittish polo pony he'd had in prep school, she refused to make eye contact. Still, she inched across the leather bench seat, never fully loosening her hold on the table.

He kept his stance wide and his center of gravity low. The last thing she needed—or he wanted—was for her to see him go down like Joe Frazier in a bout with Muhammad Ali. "Just a little bit farther."

"I'm not a moron," she gritted out between clenched teeth as she stood.

He bit the inside of his cheek to stop from grinning at her surly attitude. "No one said you were."

Sticking close together, they crossed the aisle to the

bucket seats. He waited for her to clip her seat belt closed before settling into the chair across from her. Right on cue, the jet did another midair jiggle and Ryder's olive skin turned green. She slouched down and closed her eyes, rubbing her belly.

If he didn't distract her soon, this was going to end ugly.

"Give me your foot."

"Excuse me?"

"You heard me." He curled his fingers in a come-on motion. "Unless you're chicken?"

Her eye narrowed, but she complied, sticking out one foot.

The moment he touched her warm skin, a current sizzled between them. He forgot about the jet, about the turbulence, and the fact that if they weren't fucking, they were fighting. Instead, he focused on her cinnamon perfume as it invaded his personal space, teasing him with memories of the night when he'd kissed his way down her neck. His reward that night had been her soft moans as she rubbed herself against his hard cock. But today wasn't about that. It was about making her feel safe. Even if she wouldn't admit she needed anyone's protection, he needed to give her that.

The jet bounced in midair. Ryder's muffled groan as she sank further into her seat settled him firmly back into the present.

"I promise, this will help." He popped his knuckles and flexed his fingers.

Trying his best to ignore the feel of her smooth skin under his finger or the firmness of her calf where she'd rested her leg on top of his, he unhooked the black ankle strap of her Calvin Klein sandals. The brand suited her. Unfussy. Confident. Straightforward.

Dylan's Department Store had carried the sandals two springs ago. The shoe stuck out because the buyer had over purchased and the extras had to be shipped out to other stores under the corporate umbrella that offered past year styles at a discount. The whole process had been a logistical nightmare.

"What are you doing?" Her skin tone remained less than healthy, but her voice had regained some of her signature Waterberg toughness.

"Giving you a foot massage." He slipped off the sandal and laid her bare foot on his thigh, which warmed upon contact with her skin.

"Forget it." She squirmed against his grip.

He pressed his thumbs beneath the ball of her foot, making sure to deliver just enough pressure to signal to her nerves that he meant business. "Just give it a chance." Circling his thumbs in small half-moons, he worked his way back and forth across the bottom of her foot. "It's the least I can do to help."

Her shoulders drooped and the lines around her mouth relaxed. "Oh, my God, where did you learn that? It's magic." Her eyes fluttered closed.

The reaction puffed him up on a primal level, like a caveman who'd just killed a saber-toothed tiger and had guaranteed his family's survival for another day. "Benefits of an ex-girlfriend who was a massage therapist."

Ryder cracked her eyelids open. "Ex?"

"*Uh-huh*. She was less than pleased when I returned to my WASP-y roots, as she put it." Another bit of turbulence jostled her foot out of his hand, but before she could react, he reclaimed it, rotating her ankle and smoothing his palm across the top of her foot. "We got our first tattoos together. I got a dragon. She got Che Guevara's face on her…uh…breast. I should have known then that it wasn't going to work out."

"Yeah, I don't see the hipster and Mister Corporate lasting." She laughed.

"Not by a long shot." He slid his thumbs to opposite sides

of her sole, then pushed them together again before repeating the motion vertically.

Ryder sighed and all the worry in her face melted away. "I could marry you right now."

"Is that a proposal from the woman who wouldn't return my calls?"

She flinched and every muscle in her foot tensed.

He stopped rubbing her arch. "Just a joke. I didn't mean it the way it came out." *Shit. Nice one, Harris.*

"You're not my type. Not anymore. Anyway, I just can't do relationships right now. I'm in the middle of a year of no commitments."

The news annoyed him, and he renewed his massage with more vigor. "You're sure about that?"

She winced. "*Whoa*, go easy."

"Sorry." He paused at her smooth heel and interlaced his fingers, resting them on top of her foot. It was the first time he'd really looked at her feet. Her toenails were a bright cherry red. Seeing the single dash of color was like getting a glimpse of his first girlfriend's bra in eighth grade.

"Did you kill the nail technician after your pedicure?"

"What do you mean?"

"Your girly toenails."

She wriggled her ruby-tipped toes. "Don't rat me out. I have a black color only rep to maintain."

"Your secret's safe with me." He glided his hands up and down her foot, rubbing her arch with his thumbs. "What *is* your secret?" He lowered her foot and reached for her other one. She didn't argue this time when he unsnapped the thin ankle strap and slid the sandal off her foot.

"If I told you, it wouldn't be a secret."

He held her foot aloft. "Patient confidentiality."

She gave him an assessing look, her jaw rigid, then shrugged. "Have you ever heard of a catfish scam?"

"It sounds vaguely familiar." He glided his fingers up her calf to massage the suddenly tense muscle.

"It's when someone pretends to be someone else online in order to lure in people who think they're developing an actual relationship, when in reality, it's just a scam to get money."

To him, that sounded like almost everything on the Internet. "Who would fall for that?"

"Me." She crossed her arms and yanked her foot out of his grasp.

But Devin swiped it and pulled it close again. He refused to relinquish the bodily contact, wanting the touch as much as she needed the massage. And, despite her tough-chick exterior, she did. He traced his thumbs across her instep and sixty percent of the aggression seeped out of her shoulders.

"My mom, in a typical case of Italian over-involvement after I'd broken up with the latest in a long string of loser boyfriends, signed me up for a dating website without me knowing about it."

"What made them losers?"

"My type runs…" She paused. "I mean *ran* to guys who thought straight jobs were poison, or that cheating was totally acceptable, or that my checking account should be their checking account. You get the idea. They were beautiful on the outside and empty on the inside."

"So your mom took things into her own hands."

"By the time I found out, she'd already added five potential boyfriends to a list. One was Heath."

Devin returned his thumbs to the ball of her foot and increased the pressure, slowing down his speed to combat the increased tension.

Ryder sighed. It was quickly becoming one of his favorite sounds. Damn, he liked touching her. It relaxed him…and got him harder than an oak tree at the same time.

"I wasn't about to go on a date with a complete stranger. Not without finding out more about them. Which is exactly what I told the guys on my mom's list. Some got mad. Others acted all offended. A few didn't even respond. Heath was the only one who came back with a plausible history and enough real life facts to bypass my natural skepticism."

"Like what?" Unease staked a path up Devin's spine.

"The name of a local dry cleaner he used. A picture of a Golden Retriever at a Waterberg dog park. Stuff like that. Everything seemed legit. He traveled a lot for work, so we chatted online, then we met in person and started dating for real and after about six months, I thought he was the real deal. Then he invited me to come with him on a business trip."

Devin's stomach twisted with dread. He didn't like where this was going. "What happened?"

She chewed on her bottom lip, which was already starting to swell from the abuse. "He worked for a tour company and said he could get me a great deal on the flight and hotel, but I had to give him my credit card number so he could book everything for me through the company system."

Clearly agitated, she went back to twirling a long strand of hair around a finger as she stared out the plane's small window. "I told him I'd think about it. That's when he started turning the screws. The more I hedged, the more insistent he became. I'm not an idiot. I did a little more research, using Maltese's security software. Heath had a Social Security Number, a significant online presence with photos, a blog, there was even a driver's license." She paused. "He also had a death certificate. The guy—whoever he is—had scraped the personal records of a guy from Waterburg who'd had a heart attack five years ago, to create a false identity." Her voice took on a clipped, just-the-facts tone that failed to cover the pain threading through her words. "I confronted him. He lost it, became violent. I fought back. He ran off, but not before inflicting damage. I ended up in the hospital with a broken wrist and a black eye."

Devin had smashed a lot of faces when he'd been training to be an MMA fighter. The broken noses, bloody gashes, and general destruction would be nothing next to what he'd do to the man who'd harm a woman. That the prick had hurt Ryder made Devin's vision blacken around the edges.

"Did you tell the police?"

"Hell, yes. But he disappeared like a ghost. I contacted the dating website and reported him. They flagged his file and connected him with complaints from other women. Turns out he'd been making a pretty penny fleecing women—and some men—who thought they were getting a hell of a bargain on a vacation with a too-good-to-be-true boyfriend. I'm the only one to have confronted him face-to-face."

Devin paid special attention to the pressure points in her foot. "What did your mom say?"

"I never told her or anyone else in the family."

He almost dropped her foot. "Why not? I thought you were close."

"My mom had picked him out. She'd feel responsible. I couldn't do that to her. Add to that the fact that my history of dating Grade A assholes, and that I work as an investigator at Maltese Security, so I should know better than to let a con artist into my life. How would it look to them if they realized I'd gotten mixed up with a guy like Heath?"

"Like you're human?"

"No." She shook her head. "Like a naive little girl with crappy taste in men who can't be trusted to do her job."

Devin was about to retort when the fasten-your-seat belt sign *ping*ed.

• • •

Ryder's stomach floated up and bounced against her diaphragm at the same time as the captain's voice boomed over the intercom.

"We're making our descent into The Andol Republic," the pilot said over the intercom. "Please take your seats and buckle your safety belts. According to the tower, it's seventy-two degrees and sunny today. We'll be touching down in about twenty minutes. The car is already waiting for you, Mr. Harris."

Nothing like a little reality to make her realize what an idiot she'd just been, spilling her guts to a client, leaving her as open and vulnerable as a baby pig from a kid's movie. She pulled her foot out of his warm grasp. "I'd appreciate it if you didn't mention what I told you to anyone. I should never have told you."

Straightening her spine, she braced for Devin's mockery. As the youngest of five loud Italian kids and the only woman employed by the testosterone-soaked Maltese Security, she could take it.

Devin quirked an eyebrow at her. "No one will hear it from me."

She met his light brown gaze, searching for any sign of disgust at what she'd revealed, or amusement at her expense, but all she saw was understanding. For some reason, that made the whole situation worse.

The jet swooped through a cloud bank, enveloping it in a world of thick, fluffy white that created a floating wall. They broke through it into a sky so brilliantly blue, she had to blink to adjust to the light differential. Under the cloud-dotted horizon, the deep blue ocean stretched uninterrupted as far as she could see.

The total isolation unnerved her. If they dropped out of the air right now and plummeted to a watery grave, the authorities would have a better chance of finding Amelia

Earhart's remains than the jet's wreckage. All the nervous energy she'd managed to tuck away during the nine-hour flight came screaming to the surface, twisting her lungs into circus balloon animals.

"It's going to be fine." Devin's leather-rich voice pierced her panic. "No need to be afraid."

Falling back into an emotional defensive posture, she glared at him and his lopsided smirk. "I'm not. I like flying just fine."

"Really?" His gaze dropped to her hands curled into talons around the armrests. "Is that why you're about to scar the leather?"

With supreme effort, she unpeeled her fingers from the armrest and folded her hands in her lap, just as her Nonni swore a lady should. Out of the corner of her eye, she noted ten crescents carved into the tan leather.

Devin flashed a wicked grin that did crazy things to her already turbulent insides. "The Andol Republic is a chain of five islands about one thousand miles off the coast of Chile, with Andol being the largest. That's where we'll land. In a few minutes, you'll be able to see Andol on the right side of the plane. There are three dormant volcanoes and two large craters that have become big tourist attractions. You can even have a picnic on the edge of the biggest crater."

Mesmerized by his calm, tourist-guide tone, Ryder relaxed back into the seat and gazed out the window. This time the ocean below failed to pluck her nerves. The jet made a wide turn and an island appeared, a triangle of light green in the vast blue.

"Most of the main island is grassland. Early explorers' journals reported short palm trees across Andol, but by the eighteen-hundreds, most had disappeared. No one's sure why the trees vanished, but it had a huge effect on the local population who'd been fishermen up to that point. The lack of wood for boats meant no deep-sea fishing. There was a famine and even cannibalism—lucky for us, that's not the case anymore. The islanders have done a lot to revive the palm tree population and celebrate their past history. There's even a huge festival in a few days, honoring the De Mis Promesas volcano. People dress up in traditional clothes and carve intricate designs into pineapples to mark the occasion."

The island grew larger in her window, and the floor beneath her vibrated as the pilot engaged the landing gear.

She rubbed her fingers across the indentions she'd made earlier, hoping to smooth away any residual evidence of her fear. "How many times have you been here?"

"This is my first time." Devin gazed out the window, his face a blank mask as he contemplated the endless blue. "I don't like surprises."

# Chapter Five

*"I think there is beauty in everything."*

— *Alexander McQueen*

Devin turned on his cell phone and grimaced at the email from George that popped up demanding an update. Too bad he didn't have one to give. Based on his research, Sarah should be in Andol City, either at the family farm or her favorite niece's tea shop. Their best hope now was finding her at one of the fashion shows, but those wouldn't start until tomorrow. Maybe, with a little luck, they'd track her down today, haul her onto the jet, and be back home first thing in the morning, but he wasn't going to hold his breath.

And first they had to get out of the damn airport.

Tourist season was in full throttle in The Andol Republic, with extra traffic for fashion week and the volcano festival. The customs line in the small airport, weaving along through a maze of roped-off lanes, seemed as long as the one for the newest roller coaster at an amusement park. Standing behind a young couple who were having trouble keeping their hands off each other, Devin shoved his phone back into his pocket and groaned inwardly.

"Honey, I want you to keep those shoes on tonight. I can't wait to—" The man leaned in and whispered the rest of his plans in her ear, his voice too low for Devin to catch the words. However, considering the pink flush on the blonde's cheeks, he didn't have to use much imagination to figure it out.

"I don't think you can do that to your brand-new wife." She giggled.

"Mrs. Fitzsimmons, I promise I can and will do that, and so much more." His hand rubbed the curve of her ass. "I booked the honeymoon suite at the Palm Inn so we'd have plenty of privacy."

"Next!" The customs inspector's clipped command stopped the couple before they could move into the soft-core-porn zone, and they walked to the clerk's window.

Ryder shifted beside Devin, rebalancing the weight of her overstuffed bag with its stressed zipper. Looking at her wrist, anger tightened his gut. What he wouldn't do for five minutes alone with her ex-boyfriend. He hated bullies. Growing up the son of one did that to a person.

He reached out. "Here, let me hold that for you."

She gave him the side eye. "I have more than enough muscle to heft one little bag."

He eyeballed the toned lines of her arms exposed by her filmy black tank top. His horn dog id flashed back to their night together and the way her biceps had glistened as she'd pressed her hands against his chest and ridden him. "I know very well how strong you are."

Something in his tone must have tipped her off about his mental movie, and she blushed, turning her tanned, high-boned cheeks a rosy pink. She blinked twice and the blush deepened.

Devin wasn't a betting man—at least not anymore—but he'd wager his Rolex that Ryder Falcon wasn't a woman who blushed often. Being the man who accomplished that rare feat did something weird to his insides, as though he'd just guzzled a cheap beer on an empty stomach.

Before he could think about the why behind that reaction, the newly-minted Mrs. Fitzsimmons started squawking at the customs clerk. The blonde flung her arms in the air and her husband jabbed his finger against the glass box housing the uniformed agent, who only raised an eyebrow at the tirade.

"It's our *honeymoon*, I just left the prescription bottle at home and brought the pills in the Ziploc baggie. I'm not a smuggler!" Mrs. Fitzsimmons wailed. "Carl, baby, *do* something."

Responding to his bride's call to arms, Carl slammed his open palm against the glass with a *thwack* and proceeded to try to yank the door open. Security had him kissing the linoleum and cuffed in ten efficient seconds. As they hauled Carl away, Mrs. Fitzsimmons trailing behind, Devin made a note to connect Dylan's Department Store's head of security with whoever trained the airport police.

"Next!"

• • •

Half an hour later, Devin tossed their bags into the back of a Jeep Wrangler painted a shade of hot pink that was liable to blind anyone except an eight-year-old girl. Ryder stood next to the car rental agent, chatting him up. She wasn't flirting, but judging by the way the agent stalled her with detailed explanations of how to read a map, the poor deluded fool was still keeping the faith.

"So, we're hoping to run into a friend while we're here

for fashion week." Ryder said. "She's local and just returned home a day or two ago."

"Perhaps I can help you find her." The agent puffed up his chest like a peacock—as if the guy had a candle's luck in a windstorm. "What is her name? I may know her family. It's a small island."

Devin deposited himself next to Ryder, close enough to touch her shoulder, and smiled down at the agent. Not to intimidate—well, not completely. "Sarah Molina."

The man's smile evaporated and his chest caved. "No, I don't know her."

"Are you sure?" Ryder asked, digging her elbow into Devin's side to push him away.

The man looked over his shoulder at the small tarmac behind him, deserted except for a baggage crew working at the other end. Maybe it was because of his years dealing with MMA fighters, but he could practically smell the fear rolling off the agent. It was enough to make Devin check the perimeter for trouble.

"She is your friend?" The agent crumpled the map he'd been showing her.

"More of a work associate." Ryder said, apparently sensing the man's tension, too.

"You seem like nice people," the agent whispered. "You should stay away from that family. They are dangerous."

"What do you mean dangerous?" she asked, feigning a naïve look.

"Many have come looking for Molina family members, and not all have returned." The agent backed up a few steps.

"But we need to ask her some questions," Devin said. He pulled out his wallet and took out a hundred dollar bill.

The agent's gaze locked on the greenback. "Questions?"

"She has something of mine." He held out the money.

"I see you speak our native tongue." The agent swiped the

bill and glanced over his shoulder. "Find Borja at The Palm Inn." Without another word, he jogged back to the terminal.

"Please tell me The Palm Inn is the hotel where we're staying," Ryder said.

Devin pulled out his cell phone and texted a travel change request to George's executive assistant, Suzie, so she could make the reservation change, then he climbed into the Jeep's driver's seat. "It is now."

"So, it seems Sarah was hiding more than just her embezzlement scheme." She slid into the passenger's seat and slammed the door. "If her family is the local badass clan, this whole operation just kicked it up a notch."

With that thought hanging in the wind, he hit the highway for the ten-mile drive to Andol City proper. As they drove, he rolled the idea of a Molina crime family around in his mind, and the best way to go after her, if it was true.

"I see the wheels turning in your head." Ryder twisted in her seat to face him. She wore sunglasses, but he could still feel the weight of her glare. "You can forget about it. George hired Maltese because we're good. I'm in charge of this case because I'm good. You're going to have to relax and let me take the lead."

"So, in your imagination"—he put a full slathering of prep school snob into his voice—"I'm just your driver?"

She raised her sunglasses to her forehead. "If it makes you feel better, you can add arm candy to your list of duties." She winked, and lowered her glasses.

"That doesn't fly. I'm the client, and whatever the client says, goes."

"When we set up base camp, go through that list of files on your laptop and look for the Maltese contract. You'll see it in black and white. When George signed the dotted line, he ceded primary decision-making on the case to Maltese—ergo, me." She grabbed her long, thick hair and whipped the wavy mass into a braid that fell between her shoulder blades.

"I'm not George." He flexed his fingers on the steering wheel before he bent the damn thing. "And I'm not the assistant."

"Pity. I think this case would go a lot smoother if you were." She scrolled through her notes on her tablet. "We need to hit the tea shop first." Wisps of the wavy strands whirled around her face, a few sticking to the shiny gloss of her full lips.

How could such a hot woman be so fucking annoying?

He pulled his gaze from her in time to see a beat up van that was coming toward them drift into their lane. Heart racing, he slammed his hand on the horn.

The van continued straight for them, the driver either too out of it or not giving a shit that he was about to ram another vehicle head on. Considering the horror stories Devin had heard about drivers here, it could be either one.

Devin swerved off the road, the dirt shoulder rumbling beneath the tires, and hit the gas. The Jeep bolted forward, avoiding the van by inches before leaving the bucket of bolts in the dust.

"Shit. Tell me everyone around here doesn't drive like that." Ryder tested her seat belt.

"I sure as hell hope not." Adrenaline sailed through his veins.

The first brightly-colored, single-story buildings of Andol City appeared around the bend. Something about the cheerfulness of it all calmed Devin's jittery pulse. He kept his gaze locked on the unlined blacktop road and the rolling hills beyond it. "You sure we should hit the tea shop first and not Sarah's family farm?"

If he were hiding out, he'd pick a huge tract of land to get lost on, instead of a tiny store in the heart of downtown Andol City. But it wasn't like Sarah gave a flying fuck about getting caught. Everything she'd done so far had been thrown straight in George's face, like a woman scorned.

"I went through the pictures of her office and the written inventory of her stuff." Ryder tapped her stylus on the screen and brought up a photo. "There are teapots from the same Andol City shop everywhere. This is a woman with a serious kettle addiction and almost five million dollars burning a hole in her pocket. Trust me, if she's not at the shop now, it's only because she's already been there."

He hated to admit it, but her plan made sense.

"Sarah's niece, Dominga, manages the place, so I'm guessing the staff probably won't be open to telling us if they've seen Sarah," she said.

"It's a small island. We'll find her." He turned the corner. "Anyway, it's not like she's been inconspicuous so far."

Andol City was home to fifty thousand residents and several thousand tourists every season—enough to make finding Sarah a challenge, but not impossible. Especially when she wasn't trying to hide her tracks.

Tea Time was located in a teal blue building that sat on the north corner of the tourist-clogged downtown square. Everywhere he looked, the distinctive ring-tipped Andol cats roamed the streets, free and unafraid of humans, much like the monkeys in India.

Devin parked the hot pink monstrosity of a vehicle in front of the store. The six-feet-high windows showcased shelf after shelf of delicate china teapots painted in island colors.

"I didn't realize tea was so big here." Ryder's seat belt zipped across her high breasts as it rewound into the Jeep's frame.

Devin fought to make his brain process her words, while his body processed something else entirely. "It's not, but a majority of the tourists are British, so the teapots make sense."

"Is there anything your research didn't turn up?"

Such a smartass.

He grinned despite himself. "Sarah's exact GPS coordinates."

They got out of the Jeep and crossed the raised boardwalk to Tea Time's display windows. Ryder peeked in. There was no way the woman could pass as a tourist. Dressed in head-to-toe, tight-fitting black, she looked one hundred percent badass business and zero percent vacation. What he wouldn't give to strip her out of those clothes and talk her into making it a naked vacation. His cock certainly liked the idea.

She eyeballed his reflection. "So, if this is such an open-and-shut, grab-and-bag case, why did you need Maltese Security's help?"

Guilt's strong fingers squeezed his chest like a stress ball, and he considered taking the chicken's way out. He could make up an excuse. He opened his mouth, but his tongue refused to form the lie. "You're here for the same reason that I'll go down if the merger fails."

A warm island breeze teased loose a long strand of dark brown hair from her braid. The strand batted against her locked jaw as she thinned her full lips. "Maltese is the scapegoat."

"If George has taught me anything, it's always to have a backup plan."

"Sweet guy."

Devin grunted. What could he say? It wasn't like he could deny it. George might look like a slightly slimmer, beardless Santa, but when it came to business, the man was as cold and calculating as Jack Frost—something Devin had learned firsthand as the old man's protégé.

George had taught Devin everything he knew about surviving in the ultra-competitive fashion merchandising world. He thought he'd seen cut-throat players when he played tight end at Stanford, but Dylan's Department Store's pocket-sized head buyer, Betty Webster, would have made the three hundred pound linebackers quake in their cleats. And the number one lesson George had taught him was: always watch his back. Always.

"Come on." He rested his palm against the small of her back to guide her into the tea shop. Electricity, strong and sure, surged up his arm and straight down to his dick. "Let's see if anyone inside knows where Sarah is."

Ignoring the world-weary sigh Ryder let out, he pushed open the door and marched after her. A blast of arctic-level air conditioning and the trill of a bell welcomed him into the Earl Grey-scented store. A pair of elderly women in flower-print dresses puttered around the teapot displays, while the men he assumed were their husbands loitered by the door. Each held four shopping bags in his liver-spotted hands.

Wordlessly, Devin and Ryder split up, taking opposite routes around the crowded shop. He turned down a narrow aisle and came face-to-face with a young woman in an orange Tea Time golf shirt.

Her almond-shaped eyes widened at the sight of him. "Is there anything particular I can help you find?" She swept back her long, straight black hair and revealed the name Dominga embroidered on the shirt.

*Bingo.*

He plastered on his most charming smile—the same one that had gotten Ann Ackerman to slide off her panties in the back of his Beemer during their sophomore year in prep school. "I'm sure you can."

Dominga's eyes narrowed. "You're Devin Harris. She said George would send his lackey for the money. Stay here. Aunt Sarah left you a note."

A bird could have pooped on his head and he wouldn't have been as surprised. Mouth gaping, he watched Dominga disappear behind a door marked Employees Only.

"This just feels wrong on so many levels." Ryder sidled up to him.

"Agreed." He kept his gaze focused on the door, but his body instantly hardened in some kind of Pavlovian-response to her proximity and her intoxicating scent.

"What's really going on here?"

Now, *that* was the billion dollar question. "Wish I knew."

Dominga sauntered out, handed him a pale pink envelope and, without another word, wandered off toward a pair of older women excitedly discussing a teal teapot in clipped British accents.

Clearing his throat, he bought time by slowly turning the envelope over. The soft, feminine paper made him as edgy as if he'd held a damaged grenade with a loose pin. With care, he picked at the sealed flap, then slid his thumb across the opening until he could pull the note free.

Ryder scooted in closer, her bare shoulder brushing against him.

He flipped open the note. Four sentences in blue ink were scrawled across the unlined paper.

IT FIGURES THAT HE'D SEND YOU TO DO HIS DIRTY WORK. YOU'LL NEVER GET THE MONEY BACK. LEAVE NOW OR YOU'LL PAY THE PRICE. THE STORE'S BOTTOM LINE ISN'T WORTH YOUR LIFE.

"She's looking out for us. That's comforting." Ryder's frustrated words brushed against his ear. "You go ahead and take the jet home. I'll find her and bring her back."

"I'm not going anywhere." A twitch in his left eye—the one that usually announced an oncoming migraine—started in full force. "You may be the investigator, but I'm still running the show."

Too bad it felt like the show was running him over. Exhaling a deep breath, he closed his eyes and counted to twenty. "Let's check into our rooms at The Palm Inn. We have an hour before the opening celebration for Andol Fashion

Week. It's a traditional affair with costumes. Ours will be waiting at the hotel."

He needed to get to the damn hotel, take his migraine medication, and figure out some fucking answers before another curveball hit him between the eyes.

God, he fucking *hated* surprises.

# Chapter Six

*"It's pathetic to have regrets about fashion."*

— *Simon LeBon*

Gritting her teeth, Ryder turned sideways and checked herself out in the floor-to-ceiling mirror next to the huge sunken tub in the suite at The Palm Inn that was supposed to have two bedrooms, but instead held only one large bed. By the time they'd checked in, all of the other rooms had been taken.

She couldn't deny it, her nipples looked like she'd spent the afternoon in the Siberian tundra instead of traipsing from one end of this tiny tropical island to the other. As president of the itty-bitty-titty committee, her idea of a boob support usually meant the little shelf bra in her tank tops, which she had in abundance in twelve shades of black. But the diaphanous, soft yellow sarong didn't come with a built-in bra, and the feel of the silky material against her sensitive flesh had her headlights flashing. That had to be the reason. The only other explanation was because she'd spent the day with Devin, and she wasn't willing even to contemplate the implications of that. She still wanted to smack herself for telling him about Heath, but couldn't deny that the unburdening had left her feeling lighter.

However, she still wasn't crazy enough to enjoy this outfit that was in another time zone from her comfort zone. For the billionth time in the past three minutes, she considered refusing to wear the damn thing that tied around her neck like a filmy halter dress. But that would only serve to tip off the fashionable elite gathering in the courtyard to celebrate the opening of Andol Fashion Week that something was amiss with Devin and his new personal assistant. They couldn't afford to have the gossips talking about them when they needed to get them to talk about Sarah.

Staying in hiding while the fashionistas gathered had to be driving Sarah nuts. From what Ryder had read in the brief, the older woman's ego wouldn't be able to take it. She'd have to show up. Hell, she might even be downstairs right now.

She smoothed her palms down the filmy material as if she could iron out the jumbled turns her stomach was taking.

*You can go out there like this. You don't have a choice.*

Capturing Sarah was the fastest way to get Devin Harris and his drool-inducing ass out of her life forever. And that was worth enduring the sarong, nipple hard-ons and all.

Resolve strengthening her spine, she ignored the mirror and strutted out of the safety of the bathroom. She made it three steps across the sand-colored tile floor before she came to a dead stop.

Devin lay in the middle of the king-sized bed. He'd flung one muscular arm across his eyes, highlighting his square jaw and lush lips. He wore a matching yellow sarong, but his was draped low on his narrow hips, leaving his tattooed chest on full display. The man was a brick house of painted muscle and power.

Her tongue turned to lust-flavored sawdust and an ache began to build in her core.

A series of sharp beeps sounded, and Devin rolled over and sat up with his back to her. A giant oak tree climbed up his spine, its branches covering his shoulder blades. A set of initials were carved into the finely-detailed bark near the bottom of the trunk: J.H. Whoever she was, J.H. obviously meant something to Devin.

*Don't care. Doesn't matter.*

"We gotta get rolling." Devin stretched, his back muscles undulating the tree branches like a stiff breeze. "Although, I don't know if I can face anyone I know wearing this outfit." He shut off the phone's alarm, grabbed the room key from the bedside table, and started to turn around. "I have no idea where I'm going to put this—"

His light brown eyes widened, and their black irises dilated. The muscles in his shoulders bunched, but the rest of him became as still as a statue—the kind that would put David to shame. His gaze dropped from her face, and he gulped audibly.

Tension snapped between them like a rubber band, stinging her already warm skin. Everything except for her damn nipples went soft and pliant. Like a lazy cat, she just wanted to curl around his thick thighs and rub against him.

"I don't suppose I'm really going to need this." He held up the phone, his hand shaking just a bit. "I'll leave the key at the front desk."

"Sounds like a plan." Her plan needed to be ignoring the hard body in front of her.

*Good luck with that one.*

Devin locked his jaw and brushed past her, stopping only when he'd reached the suite's door. His shoulders rose on a deep breath and he turned the knob, holding the door open.

Keeping her gaze on the diagonal pattern of the tile floor, she held her breath and hurried out into the hall speedily enough that her sarong's train floated behind her.

"Ryder." Devin's voice stopped her in her tracks and she turned. "You look really…pretty."

Warmth rushed up her chest to her hairline. Men had called her hot or fine or sexy, but they'd never called her pretty. That descriptor was saved for sweeter girls than her. Emotional necessity after the Heath debacle had required her to create a hardened, bitch-please persona, and few people ever saw past it.

But Devin had. And she had no idea what to do with that bit of information.

• • •

A bellhop led them out to The Palm Inn's large, private courtyard, overshadowed by the sleeping volcano, De Mis Promesas. Dozens of people sat at small tables scattered around the decorative brick patio. All were dressed in brightly colored sarongs of various tropical shades, the traditional garb taken upscale by the addition of enough diamonds to make even Harry Winston consider it overkill—and he'd owned the Hope Diamond.

Supermodels mixed with photographers, designers, and the lucky few able to afford the creations that would be displayed during Andol Fashion Week. Waiters carrying silver trays strolled between the groups, handing out fresh glasses of champagne, which was accepted immediately, and mouth-watering Hors d'oeuvres, which were not.

A long table sat in an open, grassy area and was covered in a beautiful white linen table cloth and dishes of exotic fruits and seafood. Ryder's stomach growled and Devin's echoed it. Considering the crowd, she doubted anyone would be elbowing her aside to get seconds at the buffet table.

A broad-shouldered man who looked as though he spent his life surfing between modeling gigs hurried to their side. "Mr. Harris and Ms. Falcon, I am The Palm Inn's manager, Borja. I'm so sorry about the room. To make up for the mix-up in accommodations for such honored guests as you, we've prepared a blessing ceremony for you. Please follow me."

"Really, it's not necessary," Devin said.

"But I insist." Borja turned and walked across the courtyard.

After exchanging a let's-just-follow-along glance with Devin, Ryder followed the man past the table and through the sparkling crowd. At the edge of the brick patio, Borja removed his shoes. She and Devin followed suit. The cool grass pricked the soles of her feet and tickled between her toes as they crossed to a tall palm tree standing alone in the volcano's dark shadow.

The other man clasped his hands together, his dark brown eyes misty with emotion.

Ryder's insides bounced around just as they did before a sparring match at the gym with a determined opponent. Anticipation, nerves, and something undefinable skittered through her veins. As if sensing her unease as he had on the jet, Devin pressed close to her side. The move turned out to be as much of a torment as a blessing, as her body responded to his nearness with a hungry yearning.

"May our own De Mis Promesas watch over you and your futures. May the gods, both old and new, grant you favor."

Borja withdrew a pair of thin bracelets from his pocket. The bracelets were made up of gold threads woven into a rope. He fastened one around Devin's wrist, then turned to Ryder. It was like being in a dream where she watched herself hold up her right arm. The gold bracelet felt warm against her skin as he encircled her wrist with the threads and fastened it.

Smiling, Borja grasped their hands and joined them under his calloused palm. "Bless you and bless your future."

A shiver danced up her spine, and she turned to Devin. Gone were the tension lines around his eyes and the grim set to his way-too-kissable mouth. They'd been replaced by something that looked a lot like awe.

"It is traditional for those who are blessed to exchange a kiss."

Devin went dead still next to her.

Borja winked and squeezed their hands. "Go on. You do not need to be shy at your own blessing ceremony."

He continued to talk, but all Ryder heard was the *wah-wah-wah* voice from the Charlie Brown TV specials.

"Kiss! Kiss!" the small group in the courtyard chanted.

"No, really," Ryder told Borja. "He's my boss. I'm his assistant. We can't do that. It's against the rules."

Borja smiled. "Don't you think it's good to try something unexpected?"

The volcano in the distance wavered a bit as the crowd's catcalls and laughter became louder. Fine. As if in a hazy dream, she leaned in and brushed her lips against Devin's. She'd give him a quick peck to silence the islanders.

He let out a strangled groan before his hands were tangled in her hair, his palms bracketing her face. The look in his eye was anything but professional—unless she counted the world's oldest profession. He lowered his lips to hers, and the earth rumbled beneath her feet.

Her insides turned to warm, electrified Jell-O. So much... everything. Heat. Passion. Danger. Lust. Hope. *Possibility*. This instinctual-level connection...*this* was why she'd never returned his calls. She had no control over it, and that scared her right down to her bright red toenails.

Another quake jostled them apart. A cheer went up from the crowd.

"De Mis Promesas approves!" Borja cheered. "A stirring from the volcano is a very great sign! But we don't want him to wake too much." He giggled. "Come now, to the feast."

Heart knocking around her chest like a bowling ball in a pinball machine, she kept her gaze trained on the tender green grass beneath her bare feet and followed Borja to the table. He seated her in one of a pair of chairs near the head of the table. Without a word, Devin slid into the one next to her. He grabbed the glass of wine already on the table and gulped it down. The crystal had barely touched the table cloth again when an older woman appeared and refilled it.

Before Borja could walk away, Ryder grasped the hotel manager's hand. "Thank you so much for the blessings. I'd love to talk to you about your beautiful island and its people."

"But, of course." He smiled, showing off the deep smile-lines bracketing his mouth. "What would you like to know?"

She and Devin warmed him up with questions about the weather and the history. Then after Borja had finished a glass of wine and leaned back in his chair, his shoulders relaxed and his eyes happy, she hit him with the real questions.

"We visited Tea Time this afternoon. I've never seen so many teapots in one spot. I understand it's owned by a local family. The Molinas."

Borja's eyes narrowed. "It is."

The two word response after his loquacious previous answers meant she was on the right track, but had to be cautious.

"Do you know them?" Devin asked.

"I don't know what information you're after, Ms. Falcon and Mr. Harris, but a blessing ceremony won't protect you from some of the worst dangers on this island." He took her hand between his calloused ones, meeting her gaze. A sliver of determination shone through the sadness she saw in his dark eyes. "Please, don't go looking for trouble. You won't find many who will help."

She squeezed his hand and slid hers from his grasp. "Trouble can't always be avoided."

"Then I will pray for you both." Borja pushed his chair back from the table and stood. "Good night." He left to mingle with the crowd.

"That got us bupkis," Devin muttered.

"Not quite. We have an ally. He's just not ready to talk, yet."

"What makes you say that?"

"He said not many will help." Certainty filled her. "He didn't say *he* wouldn't."

Devin shook his head. "You're parsing it pretty damn close."

"As my dad always said, sometimes you have to go with your gut."

Two men lumbered out of the hotel, hauling a large, heavy pot between them, and everyone at the table clapped.

"We have for you something very special." Borja told the gathered fashionistas. "This is a *curanto*. It is a mix of clams, oysters, lobster, mussels, sausage, potatoes, the potato bread *milcaos*, and *chapaleles*, which are dumplings. We make it in the traditional manner. We dig a meter-deep hole into the ground and cover it with heated stones. The ingredients are added in layers. Each layer of food is covered with Chilean rhubarb leaves. There is nothing like the *curanto* made in The Andol Republic." He spooned the *curanto* onto Ryder's plate. "Enjoy."

Spices and the scent of the sea wafted up from her plate. The heavenly taste exploded on her tongue and she couldn't stop her moan of delight. Devin tensed beside her, and out of the corner of her eye, she noticed his eye twitch had returned.

"Is it a migraine?" she whispered.

He gulped and shook his head, then shoveled the *curanto*

into his mouth like a man who'd been fasting for a week.

So, they ate, talking to the other guests and asking if anyone had seen Sarah yet, but studiously ignoring each other.

"Oh, I haven't seen her," said one designer's assistant who couldn't be a day over twenty and had snow white hair that fell in carefully arranged waves across three-fourths of her face. "But she'd never miss an Andol Fashion Week, now that she's finally home. From what I hear, she couldn't wait to come back and be a part of it. The way the locals treat her, this place is like her own little fiefdom."

"I wonder why that is…" Ryder let the statement hang, betting that, like most people, the woman wouldn't be able to stand the silence.

"I hear her son is some big muckity-muck who owns most of the island. They also own a pineapple farm outside of town." The woman shot back the last of her champagne. "Did you know pineapples grow on the ground? I always thought they came from trees."

A slightly-built man with thick-framed glasses and a handlebar mustache leaned forward. "Who cares about pineapple? I hear her son makes his money the old-fashioned way."

The girl blinked, her blue eyes as sparkly as the walnut-sized diamond pendant around her neck. "He inherited it?"

"No, he steals it." The man waggled his thick eyebrows like a Saturday morning villain on a bad cartoon show before throwing his head back and roaring with laughter. "God, you two are so gullible."

Turning away before she clocked the guy, Ryder mingled with the fashionable crowd, chatting with the guests, asking everyone about the last time they'd seen Sarah, and if they knew anything about her family. But all the while, she couldn't help but be aware of every intake of breath and shift in position Devin made next to her. Awareness settled in her belly and tightened her lungs, her destined-to-be-denied anticipation ratcheting up in intensity as the sun settled lower on the horizon. Her brain was all for pretending Devin wasn't right beside her, but her body wasn't willing to give up the fight.

"I've talked to half the people here about Sarah," Devin grumbled.

"Well, I've hit up the other half," she retorted. "And we both have jack shit. The best I've got is that she confirmed her attendance at the shows tomorrow, and that her son is the big man on the island who isn't afraid to throw his weight around—possibly in Tony Soprano fashion."

"So we're at a dead end." He rubbed the short hairs of his buzz cut.

Her fingers itched to follow his path. "Only until the shows tomorrow."

They rose to leave the party, but an older woman stopped them.

"I have something special for you, dear. You must have a taste." She uncorked a bottle of homemade wine, its clear glass container without a label, and poured Ryder a small amount. "This is for a traditional blessing toast." She captured Devin's attention with the snap of her fingers and poured him a glass. "*Salud y amor y tiempo para disfrutarlo.*"

Ryder and Devin clinked glasses and sipped the wine. Dry and warm with an aftertaste she couldn't quite place, it slid down her throat.

"You must drink the whole glass or it is bad luck." The woman pushed their glasses back up to their lips.

The rest of Ryder's wine went down like warm honey laced with a hint of anise. A flush heated her belly and climbed to her tingling breasts. "What's in the drink?"

"You don't need to worry about that. It's just an herbal mixture to help you appreciate all the blessings in your life and to let you see what your heart truly desires."

"What." Ryder's breath hitched.

"Was." Hot liquid want pooled deep in her belly.

"In." Her skin itched for Devin's touch.

"The." Her thighs buzzed.

"Drink?" Ryder's heart raced, scattering her thoughts like the flashing lights of a Fourth of July sparkler.

"Damiana for the heart to see better." The old woman got up from her seat, patted Ryder's heated cheek with a papery hand, then disappeared into the hotel.

Putting her college botany minor degree to good use, she wracked her brain trying to remember why damiana sounded familiar. Then it hit her. It was a wild shrub said to be an aphrodisiac that gave people a mild, pot-like high.

Pushing away her plate filled with decadent-smelling oysters, lobster, and albacore, Ryder accepted her current reality. She hungered for only one thing: Devin.

# Chapter Seven

*"My only interest in women's clothes is what's underneath them."*

— *Lynda Carter*

Ryder couldn't close the door to the suite fast enough. With her brain screaming "*Escape!*" she'd hightailed it back so fast she'd left her shoes in the courtyard. So what if she wanted to double dip with the hottest man she'd ever had a one-night stand with? That didn't mean she was going to. The knee-erasing need was just a pre-hangover from some crazy, volcano-blessed ceremony on a tropical island paradise.

And why, exactly, that made her want to cry or punch a wall wasn't something she wanted to think about right now.

Wanting to get as much space as possible between herself and the evening's events, she untied the filmy sarong from around her neck. It slid down her body, caressing her taut nipples and narrow hips like the reverent touch of a man's hands. And damn her black soul, she wished it was Devin's fingers trailing across her flushed skin.

The material puddled at her feet, trapping her in its mocking, cheerful circle. This was why she only wore black. Because she wasn't cheerful. Or sweet. She was cold, hard, and calculating. She had to be, and it was about time she remembered that.

Standing in only the gold bracelet and her black satin panties with her hands on her hips, she contemplated burning the stupid dress in the bathroom sink. The smoke detector's blinking green light called her back from that bit of insanity. Instead, she kicked the yellow fluff into the corner. Back in more familiar sartorial territory, she muttered a quick prayer of gratitude that at least the effects of the blessing-enhancing wine had worn off.

"I didn't realize you were so eager to get back to our room." Devin's voice warmed her like a fur coat in the middle of an August heat wave. "Everyone clapped when I got up to chase after you."

"Well, they're not here now." She whirled around, not caring that she was practically buck naked. It wasn't like he hadn't seen her completely in the flesh already.

The memory of their night together ratcheted up her body heat to face-of-the-sun levels, and judging by the tent Devin's cock made in his sarong, she wasn't alone.

A light sheen of sweat made his hard abs glisten in the dimly-lit room. The urge to lick her way across his six-pack weakened her knees. Maybe that special enhancer hadn't evaporated from her system, after all.

"God, you're beautiful." He uttered the words as soft as a prayer, and her black, strappy sandals slipped from his grip. They hit the floor with a *boom* in the silent room.

Anticipation thickened the air in her lungs, making it hard to breathe…or to think. Feeling, on the other hand, became the only thing she could do. All she wanted to do. And that loss of control scared the shit out of her. She'd been down that road before, and sure as hell wasn't getting her passport stamped for a return visit.

With deliberate care, she sauntered across the room, her bare feet slapping against the tile floor. "I'm getting my clothes and going to bed. You can take the couch."

His need was so palpable it practically reached out and touched her as she passed him to grab her black cotton tap pants and threadbare tank top from the tote in the closet. She fished out her pajamas from the stuffed bag. Ignoring the catch in her breath and the want dampening her panties, she kept her back to him and pulled the tank over her head.

"Why?" The simple word, heavy with meaning, hung between them.

"Why what?"

"Why didn't you return my calls?" Most men would have whined the question or asked with a snide edge. But Devin wasn't most men.

For the briefest of moments, she considered lying, but the truth was always a more brutal way to stop further inquiries. "Because I wanted to so badly. You were the first person since Heath that had me thinking 'what if.' I promised myself a year without any 'what ifs', without any heartbreak. So I don't sleep with anyone more than once, unless there is a very clear fuck-buddy only understanding."

"Ever?"

"Not for another four months. I gave myself a leave of absence from relationships."

Warm, strong hands gripped her shoulders and spun her around until she was practically nose-to-nose with him. "I hate that someone fucked with your head this much, but I'm not that guy."

She shrugged. "Doesn't matter, because the end result is

the same."

They stared at each other, their bodies so close his hard cock brushed her thigh. It took everything she had not to reach down, wrap her fingers around its wide base, and stroke him. His head angled downward, his mouth slightly open. One tiny move and those lips would be on hers. A few more, and his thick length would fill her up until she couldn't take any more and broke apart in his arms.

"Are you saying you're scared to sleep with me again?" Challenge sparkled in his eyes.

Her heart hitched up. A challenge was something she never let slide. "As I recall, we didn't do a lot of sleeping."

"Don't try to turn the argument around." He shook his head and placed a palm firmly on the wall beside her head, trapping her on one side but leaving a route for escape. His gold bracelet, the one that matched hers, twinkled in the dim light.

Silly man. Didn't he realize by now that she relished the battle—because she always found a way to win? She batted her eyelashes and stayed her ground. "Were we fighting?"

He cut the space between them, proof of his arousal rubbing against her slick, panty-covered folds. "There is always make-up sex."

She *tsk-tsk*ed, and used a single, determined finger to ease him back—before she came just from the casual contact with his cock. "I'm not sleeping with you again."

"Then you won't mind just kissing me." He dragged a knuckle across her bottom lip, setting off electric shocks through her body. "I've been dreaming about this sweet mouth for weeks now. Kissing it. Licking it. Watching it open as you moan my name while you come. How it would look wrapped around my dick."

Her tongue turned to powdered chalk as the rest of her dissolved into molten liquid.

"What's wrong? You're not scared of one little kiss, are you?"

She straightened her spine, pushing out her boobs until they grazed his own hard nipples. "I'm not scared of anything."

His eyes darkened and he raised his other arm, enclosing her between his sinewy, inked biceps. "Prove it."

*Oh, it was on.*

She sucked her bottom lip, drawing her front teeth across it, never losing eye contact with her challenger. The man thought he was ready. He was about to learn how wrong he was.

Her first touch came not from her lips, but from her thumb brushing his slightly parted mouth. He shivered under her fingertips and nipped her thumb. She clenched her thighs together in an effort to maintain control over the desire rushing in waves over her.

"That's not a kiss." Gravel infused the honey of his voice.

"No." She brought her mouth millimeters from his. "This is."

Giving in to the wicked temptation he offered, she pushed her hands against his shoulders, shoving him against the opposite wall. Her mouth was on his before the shock of her sudden move could possibly register in his brain. This wasn't just a kiss, it was a full frontal attack. She melded her lips to his, not waiting for an invitation to sink her tongue into his luscious mouth, but instead pushing her way in. He tasted of fruity wine, seafood, and all the deliciously bad things her mother had warned her about with boys. Dragging her hands upward, she relished the coarse texture of his close-cropped hair against her palms. She plastered her hungry body against his muscular frame, rubbing against the steel between his legs.

Riding high on passion, she wanted nothing more in the world than to follow through with her body's demands, ride him until he couldn't come any more, fall into a sweaty heap beside him to sleep, and then wake up a few hours later to do it all again. His personal mixture of raw sensuality and almost animalistic single-mindedness was the perfect fit for her own single-minded needs. She'd known it the minute his hands had roamed across her ass on the dance floor the night they first met—Devin was the man who'd make her let down her guard, forget the bitter lesson she'd learned last summer, and lose control.

That couldn't happen.

Easing back from his throbbing cock and intoxicating kiss, she fought to steady her breathing and get the world back on an even keel.

"Close." He flipped her around so her back pressed flat against the wall, cupped her ass, and lifted her until she had no choice but to wrap her legs around his narrow waist. "But let me show you how it's really done."

His dick rocked against the crotch of her soaked panties, slow and steady, so unlike her heartbeat. He didn't seek out her kiss-swollen mouth, instead he zeroed in on the base of her throat, sucking and nipping at the sensitive flesh. Her moan escaped before she could even attempt to hold it back, the fire burning through her too fast and hot to deny.

He licked his way up her throat, bringing his mouth against her ear. "You make me so fucking hard." He ground his cock against her, squeezing her ass cheeks in his firm grip. "This is what you do to me every time I so much as think about you. And if I don't stop, I'm going to come in my boxers instead of buried deep inside you, which is the only place in the world I want to be right now."

Reason exploded into a pile of well-intentioned ash. Her body was about to get what it so desperately wanted. "Put me down."

He stilled against her, their position as intimate as it could be with her still in panties and him in the sarong clinging for dear life to his hips. He knocked his forehead against the wall but released his hold.

She glided down his body until her feet touched the tile, icy cold compared to the heat roiling through her body, and pushed him back several paces so that the back of his knees nearly hit the bed. Not giving him time to recover, she swept her leg behind his and knocked him down onto the pale blue comforter. The air in his lungs *whoosh*ed out. Another man, she might have worried about, but Devin played—and worked out—just as hard as she did.

One hard yank, and his sarong joined hers in the corner. Another tug, and his boxers followed suit. He lay flat on his back, never moving a muscle while she stripped him, but the look in his light brown eyes was anything but docile. He deliberately slid his right hand across the tribal design covering his pecs, over the flat landscape of his abs and stopped only when he wrapped his long fingers around the base of his shaft.

"I think you need more practice to perfect your kissing skills." The devilish gleam in his eyes dared her to make the next move as he rubbed his cock in long, slow strokes.

Her nipples were hard enough to rip through the thin cotton of her tank top, and the urge to sink to her knees and follow the movement of his hands with her tongue hit with the force of a semi plowing into a plywood derby cart. But a single shred of self-preservation held her back. *Her game. Her way.*

Determined to maintain the upper hand, she strutted to the edge of the bed, lowered herself, and planted her knees on either side of his corded thighs. She wrapped her hands around his wrists and brought them up over his head as she crawled over him.

"Be a good boy and you might get your wish." She ran her hands down his tattooed arms, keeping herself positioned so that her center hovered directly above his hard cock but didn't touch it. "I could spend hours just tasting you. The question is, where to lick first?"

She lowered her head to his pecs and traced the round lines of ink that ended like the yellow brick road at his nipple. She lapped at the flat, dusky nub, drawing him into her mouth and sucking.

His moan echoed in the room, and he wriggled beneath her, bringing his dick into direct contact with her.

Releasing him and raising herself higher, she flicked his nipple and then followed her hands as they traveled up his arms and wrapped around his wrists. The position resulted in her still hidden breasts dangling an inch above his panting mouth, his humid breaths pushing the well-worn material against her overheated flesh. Teasing him had become her own torture.

He angled his head up, sucking her breast through the tank top, engulfing the small mound into his mouth. His tongue circled her almost painfully hard nipple.

"You're not being a very good boy right now." Her voice shook almost as much as her thighs.

"That"—he broke free of her grasp—"is because"—he gripped her hips, rolled her over, and took up residence between her splayed legs—"I'm not good." He grasped the thin cotton material of her tank top. "And I'm definitely not a boy." He yanked the black cloth, ripping it in half and exposing her breasts to his feasting eyes. "Sweet God, woman, you are going to be the death of me."

The reverence in his eyes as he stared down at her shifted something deep inside, and an emotion as close to shyness as she'd ever experienced tickled up from her toes. Her hands itched to cover herself as she lay open and vulnerable beneath him. Then he lowered his lips to hers, and every thought evaporated.

His tongue swept inside her mouth, teasing her until she

was a writhing mix of want and need. She ran her hands up his thighs, the curly, coarse hair springing against her palm, and didn't stop until she had both hands on his firm ass. Pulling him downward, she refused to stop until his cock lay nestled against her core, the damn panties blocking his entrance.

His hands were everywhere at once, caressing her breasts, skimming across her stomach, and finding their way between her panties and her silky folds. He dipped a finger into her entrance, his thumb circling her attention-starved clit, and her spine bowed so sharply she almost bounced him off the bed.

He regained his balance and his mouth found a home, kissing its way from her right nipple to her belly button.

"I want to rip these silky things off you, too."

"How about you just take them off, instead?"

He answered with a growl and dipped his head lower, taking the elastic band of her panties between his teeth and dragging them down her legs. Pushing her legs back open as wide as they could go, he kissed and licked his way up her calves and thighs, not stopping until he arrived at the center of her need, where his tongue and fingers worked in concert. Her thighs trembled as the tension within her tightened, blocking out everything except his mind-blowing efforts between her legs. Then, her muscles locked and she came undone.

"I want to be inside you so bad it's killing me, but I don't have a condom."

"Not a—" She swallowed the word "problem." She always kept a condom in her wallet. For her, it was just wise planning, but some men would get all judgmental about a woman being proactive. Not that they thought bad things about themselves when they shoved a condom in their wallet.

But Devin had already proven himself different from most of the men she'd dated, and really, did she even care what he thought of her? It wasn't like there was relationship potential here. Extending her arm, she swiped her wallet off the bedside table and took out the condom. The foil package glimmered in the honeymoon suite's dim light.

"If you weren't on this whole no-commitments-for-a-year thing, I'd be down on one knee right now." He nuzzled her neck.

"Watch out, soon enough you might be, anyway."

He laughed and rolled on the condom.

Taking back control, she pushed him onto his back and raised herself, centering her opening over his straining cock. Bracing herself with her palms flat on his hard chest, she lowered herself, inch by inch, until she enveloped him fully. After that, instinct and need took over. They moved together in a primal rhythm, both lost in the absolute pleasure of the moment. The tingling started low in her belly, growing and morphing within her as she arched her back to allow him deeper.

"Devin!" she called out just as her climax hit.

A few breaths later, he gripped her thighs, pulling her down hard against him, and exploded with his own orgasm.

She collapsed on top of him before rolling onto her side, sated and satisfied. Beside her, Devin rolled onto his stomach. Even destroying an opponent in the ring never felt this good.

The full moon's light filtered through the sliding glass door, illuminating his muscular back. The tree tattoo looked even more impressive up close. She traced her finger across the detailed limbs and down the thick trunk that traveled the length of his spine.

She outlined the J.H. with her short nail. "Who's J.H.?"

The muscles in his back hardened, and he rolled onto his back, shutting off her view of the tattoo. "That's not a story for tonight." He pulled her close, so her head fit in the curve of his shoulder, and brushed his lips across the top of her head.

Her eyes fluttered, post-coital exhaustion zapping her curiosity. Closing her eyes, she promised herself that she'd rest for a minute, then figure out what to do next. But her plan lost its luster when he intertwined his fingers in hers, snuggled up into the spoon position, and fell into a half-snoring sleep. Basking in the warmth of his embrace, she gave up on her former strategy and let her breath deepen.

There'd be time enough to freak out tomorrow.

# Chapter Eight

*"I don't design clothes, I design dreams."*

— *Ralph Lauren*

A death metal drummer was going to town in Devin's head, crashing the cymbals loud enough that the sound vibrated down his spine and exploded in his kidneys. Peeling his eyes open, he slapped his palm against the alarm-blaring phone on the night stand. The blessed silence was broken only by the sound of a nearby shower running. Confusion muddled his foggy brain. Waking up in a strange room wasn't completely foreign, but it had been years since it had happened.

He brought the room into focus and scanned the area. Pale blue walls dotted with landscape paintings featuring beaches and palm trees. An overhead fan pulling in the salty air and ocean breeze from the open French doors leading to a small, private patio. Soft yellow material crumpled up in a corner. His gaze froze, an image of Ryder arching her back in ecstasy burned itself into his brain, and he became painfully aware of his morning wood tenting the sheet.

The shower turned off.

He had about sixty seconds to melt his boner or walk bow-legged past Ryder to the bathroom. He did not want to do that.

Gathering the little bit of mental focus he had at the moment, he zeroed in on all the crap going on in his life right now.

The merger of the year that would rock the fashion world rested on quietly catching Sarah Molina and recovering the money she'd embezzled.

He went to half-mast.

If he couldn't make that happen, he'd be tossed out on his ass and labeled a disappointment, just like his old man had predicted when he'd started with Dylan's Department Store. Just like he had failed to protect his little brother, James.

Devin's hard-on turned into a large speed bump under the sheet.

Oh, yeah, and he'd just had mind-blowing sex—again—with the woman who'd fucked him and then wouldn't return his calls. The only reason Ryder had wanted him last night was because of some crazy island aphrodisiac an old woman had mixed in their wine. It didn't have a damn thing to do with him.

That did it. He deflated until he was practically a eunuch.

Ryder emerged from the bathroom with a white towel wrapped around her body. Her long, wet hair hung down her back. Drops of moisture glistened on her shoulders.

His mouth transformed into a highway in the desert seventy miles from a gas station. God, the woman was going to fuck him up, and he was so stupid that he looked forward to the carnage.

She gasped and slammed to a stop. "Sorry, I thought you

were still asleep." Her voice trembled a bit and her hands crossed in front of her body, locking the fluffy white terrycloth in place.

"Nope." *Way to state the obvious, dude.*

"Well…" She gave him a wild-eyed look and swiped some clothes from the closet. "I'll just get dressed now." She shuffled backward, stopping when her back *thunk*ed against the bathroom door, exhaling an *oof*.

"You okay?"

She snorted. "Peachy keen." Then she scurried into the bathroom, shoving the door shut behind her.

They sure were a pair of articulate people.

He fought the urge to smother himself with a thick pillow. What would he say to her, anyway? *I know last night only happened because of the spiked wine, but I'd like it to happen again.* That didn't sound desperate or pathetic at all. He groaned.

Time to get his balls out of Ryder's purse and man up. They'd fucked. It was good. It wouldn't happen again. So what? It wasn't as if he cared.

Bravado pumping him back up, he sprang off the bed and pulled on his boxers.

"I'm going to go grab some breakfast. You want me to bring you back anything?" Ryder's voice had regained is firm footing in badass chick territory, which made sense since she was back in her usual all-black uniform of skinny cigarette pants and a sheer black blouse with a tank underneath. Noticing a woman's outfit was second nature to him by now—the pro and con of living and breathing women's fashion for the past decade.

"Breakfast?" His stomach rumbled. "Grab me something with lots of protein. We've got to nail down Sarah Molina today at the fashion show. I could use an energy boost."

Ryder picked at the collar of her blouse, right next to the

spot where he'd done his damnedest to mark her last night. Heat rushed up his body at the memory of their battle for dominance. Be it the bedroom or the boardroom, few people ever challenged him. He'd never experienced such a rush of excitement at the prospect of battle as he had last night with Ryder.

"Protein it is." She gave a curt nod and slipped out the door.

Looked like they were going to ignore the smell of hot sex still hanging in the room. He was good with that. Course he was. He was Devin Harris—jock turned fashion executive; rich kid made good; a man who rarely spent a night alone unless he wanted it that way. His hangover explained the tightness in his throat. No way was it because of her.

He strolled toward the bathroom, stopping when his toes brushed the filmy yellow material puddled on the floor. Without thinking twice, he bent down and grabbed the soft sarong she had worn. Her sensual scent teased his senses, and his body responded with an instant hardening. After breathing in one last, deep lungful, he let the fabric slide out of his grasp.

• • •

"I swear to God, Sylvie, if you breathe a word of this to Tony, I will never come back and you'll have to explain to my mother why her baby daughter is living on an island where they probably make lasagna with cottage cheese." The cramp in Ryder's stomach had nothing to do with hunger and everything to do with the hot guy she'd left in the suite.

A staticky silence crackled from her cell phone as she paced in front of the ice machine. A *crash* sounded behind her and she whipped around, half expecting to see Devin and his drool-worthy six-pack leaning against a wall. Instead, the hall remained empty. More banging emanated from the ice machine as it dropped a fresh load of ice into the freezer.

High-strung? Her? Not at all.

"Yeah, yeah, calm down. I promise not to breathe a word of it to your brother, even if he is asleep in the next room and would turn about twenty shades of pissed off if I told him you were sleeping with a client."

Her brother's live-in girlfriend and her best friend or not, Ryder was going to kill Sylvie.

"*Slept*. Past tense. It will not happen again."

"That sure was convincing, said no one, ever."

Ryder shrugged her shoulders. "I don't even like him." Good thing she was leaning against the ice machine because her black pants were about to spontaneously combust.

"*Uh-huh*."

"He's just so…"

"Hot? Good in bed? Sex on a stick?"

*Yes. Yes. And yes*. "You are not helping, Sylvie."

"Look, I remember what you were like after you two hooked up and you ditched him like Cinderella after the ball. You were a mopey and snarly woman, and if I didn't love you, I'd have conked you over the head with my favorite Coach bag. Something about this guy just does it for you. Maybe it's time you started listening to that little voice inside you. Your instincts weren't totally off with any of your exes—even with Heath. You went with your gut and you found out the truth."

The idea of doing that scared and thrilled her. Could she trust herself again? Was she on target with Devin?

"Anyway," Sylvie chuckled. "You're in a tropical island paradise with him, you might as well go for broke."

Ryder's stomach fluttered. "Thanks for the reminder."

"What are friends for?"

"Chocolate ice cream and booze."

Sylvie laughed. "Yeah, I'm good for that, too."

"I have a feeling I'm going to need both when I get back

to Harbor City. Thanks for everything, Sylvie."

"No problem." She sighed. "But think about what I had said, okay?"

Thinking about Devin wasn't the problem. The fact that she couldn't *stop* thinking about the hotness sitting in the suite, now *that* was a huge problem.

"Before you go, there's one more thing I have to tell you." Sylvie paused.

Ryder's sixth sense for trouble perked up, and she held her breath, knowing whatever she heard next would rock her world.

• • •

The egg white omelet could have been made from painted cardboard for all Devin could taste. All the brain cells not connected to basic functions, like remembering to breathe, were busy making sure he didn't say or do anything stupid while sitting across from Ryder at the wrought iron table on the patio.

Over her left shoulder, he could see white-tipped waves rolling onto the beach about ten yards from where they sat silently during the most tension-filled breakfast he'd ever experienced. Shit, telling his father to go ahead and disown him hadn't been as nerve-wracking.

If he could turn down the Harris billions without blinking an eye, surely, breaking bread with Ryder Falcon was no big deal. He just needed to explain that last night was a freak—and freaky hot—occurrence that couldn't happen again. The irony of being the one to say those words after the way she'd ditched him after their previous night together should have been a kick-ass victory.

It wasn't.

"So…" His brain tried to catch up with his mouth, but it

was slow rolling. "How's your fruit and yogurt?"

"Good." Ryder sucked the last bit of Greek yogurt off her spoon and Devin bent his fork, the metal digging into his thumb.

He must have groaned out loud because her lips started to twitch and she snorted a half giggle. "Let's just get it out there, okay? We had sex. It was awesome, but it shouldn't have happened." Her brown eyes locked in on him as an ocean breeze tumbled her hair. "We're both grown-ups. We can move forward from here."

*It was awesome.* The phrase stood out as if she'd spray painted it on the table. She thought sex with him was *awesome*.

She stared at him for a moment with her wide brown eyes as if she expected him to argue, to protest, but his brain was too scrambled to come up with anything. His gaze followed a long strand of silky brown as it tangled around her blouse buttons.

"Glad you see it that way," she uttered, her tone sharp.

What had he missed? She'd just blown him off. Again.

Her spoon clanged against the parfait glass rim as she released it and then crossed her arms, dislodging the hair that had snared his attention…and his libido.

The woman twisted his brain. Not sleeping with her was the best thing for both of them with so much on the line. He *did* see it that way. At least his big head did. The little head had other ideas. On automatic pilot, he shoveled the last bite of omelet into his mouth and followed it with the last gulp of orange juice.

"We'd better get moving." Ryder's chair screeched against the cement patio as she pushed back from the table and stood.

*Keep it professional and all business.* He could do this. Couldn't he?

• • •

Ryder stopped halfway into the room and waited for Devin to close the sliding glass door. As soon as it clicked shut, she put the bed between them, needing the mental safety a physical barrier provided. Then she glanced down at the rumpled covers, still twisted from last night's activities, and heat singed her from the toes up. Sylvie was wrong. Trusting her instincts was the last thing that should happen.

Devin's quiet chuckle from the other side of the room meant her reaction hadn't gone unnoticed.

Great.

She hot-stepped it away from the bed and toward him. "I talked to my friend Sylvie this morning. She's a fashion blogger, the High-Heeled Wonder."

"Sylvie Bissette, right?" He strolled closer, his pace as deliberate as his words. "Wasn't she the one who had that crazy stalker a while back?"

"That would be the one." A demented fashion insider-turned-whack-a-do had become obsessed with outing Sylvie's top secret blogger identity and then killing her. Yeah, the stalker had been a real piece of work, to put it mildly. The only good thing to come out of the whole situation had been Tony and Sylvie falling in love.

"Does that happen a lot?"

"Stalker cases?"

"No." Devin stopped within arm's reach. "Maltese Security personnel getting involved with a client."

Ryder stumbled over her own feet and wobbled in midair. Just as gravity grabbed hold of her, Devin wrapped an arm around her waist and pulled her back against his hard chest. His hand lay flat against her stomach, fingers spread wide. Electricity jumped from his fingertips to her skin, strong enough that she might well have been naked instead of wearing a simple cotton tank. The power of attraction coursed through her and raced across her skin, making her breathless and lightheaded.

Heat sizzled through her veins. It was too much in one breath and not enough in the next. She felt ready to combust on the spot. Which was why she had to put as much space between them as possible. Too bad forcing her legs to move had become beyond her capability.

She had to get the words out before her brain short-circuited. "Someone told Sylvie that Dylan's Department Store is about to tank financially."

He jumped backward, as if her words had burned him. "And how in the hell would someone know that?" Accusation lay heavy in his tone.

But she noticed he hadn't denied it. All the soft fuzzies evaporated in a second. "W-what?"

"Up until you dropped your four-point-seven million dollar bomb on me in Harbor City, it seemed that George was the only one who knew that bit of information. Hell, even I didn't have a clue that it's as bad as it is. This could ruin the MultiCorp deal."

She rounded on him and planted her hands on her hips. "Are you blaming the leak on *me*?"

Anger had painted him scarlet. Before he could open his accusing mouth, a knock sounded at the door. She stormed over and yanked it open.

"Good morning, Ms. Falcon." A bellboy held a large envelope with her name and a Maltese Security return address. His eyes widened when he got a look at her, and he took a step back. "This just came for you," he said, his voice wobbled as he handed the package to her. "The messenger said it was urgent."

"Thank you." She shut the door and ripped open the envelope.

She'd told Tony to back off. If he was trying to micromanage things on top of her having to deal with the asshole across the room, this case could get ugly. The Thanksgiving when Uncle Sal had tried to stab Sammie Jr. with a cannoli would have nothing on her throw-down with her big brother when she saw him again.

Inside the envelope were several eight-by-ten color photographs and a piece of paper. She pulled out the photos and her pulse went into overdrive. *Holy shit*. Obviously, the return address was bogus.

The first showed her and Devin standing in line at customs. The second showed them outside the tea shop. Her vision darkened around the edges as fury swirled inside her. But she couldn't give in to it. Not yet.

"What it is? Are you okay?" Devin hustled to her side and tried to put an arm around her.

She easily sidestepped the move. "I'm fine." The bastard had been just about to accuse her of submarining her own case before the bellboy arrived, and now he wanted to comfort her?

Fuck. That.

She blinked until she could focus on the pictures again. In the third, she and Devin were holding hands during the blessing ceremony. The forth showed them in bed, making love, taken through a crack in the curtains. Devin was embracing her in the fifth shot, his muscular arms pulling her close.

Her hands shook and she fought the urge to rip the glossy paper to shreds. But they were evidence. She might be able to find something in the angles or in a reflection to lead her to the bastard who'd taken them. And then that person would feel the full impact of her wrath.

Without a word, she passed the pictures to Devin and opened the single sheet of pale pink paper.

Ms. Falcon,

Consider this your last warning. You see how easy it

IS FOR US TO GET CLOSE TO YOU. IF YOU VALUE YOUR LIFE, YOU'LL GO HOME NOW.

It ended there without a signature, but she didn't need one to know who'd sent it.

"What the fuck?" He tossed the pictures on the bed's rumbled sheets before fisting his hands.

"The images aren't grainy enough to be a telephoto lens. One of Sarah's lackeys must have been practically sitting in our laps."

"Jesus Christ." He started to pace the room. "How did we not notice that?"

The previous day rolled through her mind. The car on the road from the hotel. The wine at dinner. The almost uncontrollable urge to touch Devin after she'd drunk it. Her jumbled thoughts skittered to a stop. No one else had drunk from the special bottle.

"Maybe it was a setup. The bad driver in the van. The old woman with the wine?" The possibility made her muscles twitch with the need to move. To jab. To take out the bastard who'd just fucked with the wrong chick. "Sarah's been harassing us since we stepped off the plane."

Clenching her jaw, Ryder slowly counted to ten, timing her breaths so they lasted as long as each number, until a familiar calm loosened her muscles. Paulie had taught her a pre-fight routine to clear her mind, and she followed it now. She closed her eyes, released the fists her hands had formed, and pictured an empty ring. Her domain. Her home. No one fucked with her there.

"She doesn't realize it yet, but Sarah Molina just made a grievous error." Ryder opened her eyes. "She made it personal."

# Chapter Nine

*"Creativity comes from a conflict of ideas."*

— *Donatella Versace*

Andol Fashion Week didn't have the glitz and glamor of Paris or New York, but fashionistas from all over South America and even Europe packed into luxury homes and five-star resorts hastily converted into fashion destinations where six-foot-tall models strutted down narrow runways showcasing the best the continent had to offer. The clothes were on display, but all the ladies-who-lunch could talk about that morning were the thieves who'd hit the city's main hotel and swiped enough diamonds to fund a trip to the moon.

Ryder could give a shit if some ultra-rich women lost a few baubles that were no doubt insured. She'd hauled her ass halfway across the island for one reason only: to find Sarah Molina. A confirmed fashion junkie who'd been a part of the fashion world for three decades, there was no way she'd miss out on the continent's premier fashion event.

Walking up the stone pathway to a covered Zen garden, her kitten heels clicking on each flagstone, Ryder scanned the small groupings concentrated near the three bars placed strategically around the potted bonsai trees. These shows never started on time, allowing even the latecomers like her and Devin time to see and be seen. Her earlier rage had congealed like mozzarella cheese on a day-old slice of pizza, leaving her mind free of the red haze coloring her vision. She scanned the glittering crowd as she circled the empty runway, searching for Sarah's distinctive ebony bob. She spotted plenty of blondes, a handful of brunettes, and even the occasional white, but no bob. The lack of results turned her last nerve into a tiny nub of discontent and free-floating aggression. Well, that and the frustration of pretending she was Devin's happy little assistant even though she wanted to knock him in the nuts for thinking she'd leaked the news about the store's financial troubles.

A shadow fell across her path. She didn't have to look up to know the most annoying man in the world had stopped beside her. A tingling up her spine had told her he was near long before he darkened her sight lines.

"Do you see her?" The intensity in Devin's hushed words made a mockery of his casual stance and the loose way he held a champagne flute.

She shook her head as a short man in a blue seersucker suit rushed toward them. Immediately on guard, she pivoted and braced her shoulders in case of attack. He had a paunchy belly, teeth so white they were nearly florescent, and a bulbous nose that would make a perfect first target. She rose onto the balls of her feet, keeping her muscles loose but ready.

The man started talking before his feet even stopped moving. "Mr. Devin Harris, please allow me to introduce myself. I am Louis Pucci, The Andol Republic's cultural minister."

She relaxed back onto her heels, wishing she could exhale the fight-or-flight adrenaline rush from her veins instead of having to let it tweak through her system, making her muscles contract under her black lace sleeves.

"So good to meet you." Devin shook Louis's hand. "We've been impressed with the setup for the shows today."

The other man beamed. "Thank you, we are most proud of our South American geniuses." He turned to Ryder. "Madam, I apologize for so rudely interrupting your conversation, but I could not let an opportunity to talk to Mr. Harris go by."

"That's not a problem. This"—Devin turned to Ryder—"is my assistant, Ryder Falcon."

Louis' smooth fingers clasped hers and he brought them up to his lips. "We are so pleased you are both here with us enjoying the wonderful designs. Let me take you to your seats." He walked them to the chairs lining a raised, sixteen-feet-long catwalk. "I made sure you have premium seats. We really are hoping you find a local designer or two to feature prominently at Dylan's Department Stores across the globe when the merger goes through."

"That is the goal today." Devin's voice had a breezy tone, but his left eye twitched.

Muscle spasm or something more? She didn't give a shit. Her job was to track down Sarah, not be Devin's babysitter, and she refused to give him an inch after this morning. The only nursing she'd be doing would involve a grudge—or a bottle of tequila.

"I hope you have found our country pleasing so far." Louis stopped in front of a pair of front-row seats located three-fourths of the way down the runway and held out his hand.

Again, Devin shook the man's hand, but his gaze flitted around the gathering. "It is beautiful here."

"Wonderful." Louis executed a short bow toward Ryder. "If there's anything you need, please do not hesitate to call upon me."

"There is one thing." She ignored Devin's censorious look. He wasn't running this investigation and it was time he realized that. "We're hoping to chat with Sarah Molina while we're here. You haven't seen her yet, have you?"

"No, *señorita*." His posture stiffened and a vein quivered against his otherwise smooth forehead. "But if I do, I'll be sure to let her know you're looking for her." He took three quick steps back, not bothering to wait for a reply.

After practically fawning over Devin, now he couldn't ditch them fast enough. Alarm bells clanged in Ryder's head, but she wasn't about to let him get away that quickly.

"Do you know her well?" She gave him her best just-a-dumb-employee eye flutter.

He paused, one foot caught mid-step, hanging in the air. "I do. Her family and mine have been close friends for generations."

"How lovely," she gushed.

He returned her smile, but the dull flatness in his hard eyes sent a chill down her spine. "Indeed."

Devin must have felt it, too, because he inched toward her until he was close enough for the heat from his body to dissipate the frigidness the cultural minister inspired.

Annoyed at the relief she felt, she stepped away from him and closer to the other man. "Could I bother you to take my card, so you can reach me when you see her?"

Louis's smile held about as much warmth as the Arctic Circle. "Of course."

"You are too kind." She handed him a white business card that only listed her name and her cell phone number.

He pocketed the card, shook Devin's hand once more, and left as fast as his little feet would take him to mingle with the other guests wandering around looking for their seats.

Watching him go, she took the opportunity to cast a surreptitious glance at those gathered close by. There were South American versions of Harbor City society's great dames in color-matching looks from their wide-brimmed hats to their spike-heeled sandals. Men and women who obviously believed in the power of fashion-with-a-capital-F dotted the landscape and were dressed in avant-garde touches—including one woman with a tree-branch fascinator that curved forward to cover half her face. In between those extremes were the "It" girls and fashion forward boys who were here not only to see, but to be seen. It was a people-watching paradise.

But the one person she wanted to see remained hidden.

Reaching inside his jacket, Devin pulled out a pair of aviator sunglasses and put them on before sitting down. "Look, about what happened at the hotel room earlier. I—"

A painful tightness gripped her throat, making her response scratchy. "It doesn't matter."

"It does." He twisted in his chair, turning away from the crowd.

"No." Her grimace projected back at her from his sunglass's reflection. "We got caught up in the whole island vibe or were drugged, maybe both. Everything just righted itself back to the natural order of things. But I *didn't* leak the story and you damn well know it."

"You're right." He paused. "About almost all of it."

Everything inside her head screeched to a halt. "What do you mean *almost*?"

"Well, there!" A voice boomed between them.

Ryder jerked her focus away from Devin, annoyance and the interruption making her snarl. She did a double-take at the giant of a man standing in front of their chairs.

He was the tallest person she'd ever seen not CGIed

into a scifi movie. He had to be just shy of seven feet tall, and that wasn't counting his purple four-inch platform boots. He'd topped his summer white suit with a caplet and a paisley fedora. He looked like a demented villain from one of her nephew's cartoons.

Judging by Devin's stiff posture and vein-popping forearms, he wasn't pleased to see this newest arrival.

"Imagine seeing you in The Andol Republic, Harris," the man drawled.

"Nigel." Devin slathered the name with distaste. "I didn't know you were going to be here."

The interloper plopped down in the empty seat to Ryder's right. "Well, when I heard the wolf of the fashion world was here, how could I miss it?" He pulled out a purple paisley pocket square and dabbed his forehead.

Devin stared straight ahead, working his jaw like a grinder. "What do you want?"

Ryder had the distinct impression that unless Nigel was looking for a swift kick in the ass, he was so out of luck. Damn, if only she had a bucket of popcorn to go with the show.

"You know." Nigel rolled his shoulders. "A little of this. A little of that."

"Go look for it elsewhere, then, because I've got nothing to say to you."

Nigel chuckled, seemingly less than intimidated by Devin's snarling. "So, I shouldn't even try for a quote about how Dylan's Department Store is circling the toilet bowl? The word backstage is that you need money—bad. I hope you aren't so desperate for cash that you turned jewel thief. Half the people here are wearing fake jewels after thieves hit the local hotels last night."

Ryder's toes curled in her kitten heels. What a piece of work. It was one thing for her to be pissed at Devin, but quite another for some random dude to hurl insults at her client.

She ignored the little voice whispering inside that she'd never been bothered before when that happened with any of her other clients. Her knuckles cracked as she flexed her fingers.

Standing up, Devin loomed over Nigel's sitting form. "I always knew you had questionable taste. I didn't realize until right now that you had questionable survival skills, too."

"Oh my, did I annoy the wolf?" Nonplussed, Nigel leaned back in his chair and swiveled in her direction. "Is this your red riding hood? Is she in mourning for her grandmother or just sartorially challenged?"

She nailed him with her best bitch-please look. "I'm Mr. Harris's personal assistant."

"Ryder Falcon meet Nigel Mintus, former style maker and now... What little paper are you working for now?" Devin asked.

"I'm the fashion editor for *The Daily Guardian*."

"Which comes out weekly." Devin smirked.

She couldn't help the giggle that escaped. That burn served the asshole right.

"An unfortunate development," Nigel snarled, then shot back, "Does your parole officer know you've left the country?"

She clamped her mouth shut to keep her jaw from hitting the floor. Questions ran though her head, each led by a big *what the fuck*.

She'd searched Devin's background, looking for any bit of negative information she could find, and had never come across any criminal charges, let alone a conviction. She'd even pulled in Carlos, the Maltese Security computer guru, telling him to look up Devin's background. Carlos could hack into the nuclear defense system if he wanted, but he hadn't found shit on Devin. Who did he know to get his record wiped cleaner than Nonni's pantry?

"I don't have a parole officer." Devin stiffened and his

hands formed firsts, but he kept them lowered to his sides. The effort cost him, though, because his face turned as red as Sunday gravy.

"Oh, did I strike a nerve?" Nigel stood, raised an eyebrow, and pursed his lips into a duck face imitation. "Doesn't your… ahem…*personal assistant* know you killed a man and nearly destroyed another? I always forget, did you kill your brother or the other teenager?"

All of the air whooshed out of Ryder's lungs, leaving them aching. She whipped her head around to look at Devin. All the healthy color had fled his face.

Reaching down, he grabbed Nigel by the shirt front and yanked him out of the seat. "Get out of here before I shove one of those boots so far up your ass your teeth will be bedazzled."

Ryder sprang to her feet, squeezing between the two men. The people around them fell silent, then the buzzing began as everyone whispered and tapped their thumbs against their phone touch screens, all wanting to be the first to get out the news. Devin released his hold on the other man and took several steps backward, everything about him as tense as a lion ready to pounce.

"I'm shaking here." Nigel buffed his manicured nails against his jacket. "You better watch your manners. I'd hate to have to tell Sarah about your boorish behavior. You know she'd feel obligated to report it up the chain to George."

"So, where is she?" The words tumbled out of Ryder's mouth as her gaze darted around the crowd, searching for the diminutive older woman and coming up empty.

Nigel waved his hand in the air. "She's holed up at her family pineapple farm, recovering from the party she hosted there last night for the top designers." He smiled condescendingly at them. "That's right, I didn't see you there. So sorry you didn't rate an invitation."

The DJ stepped into his booth and a second later, a fast-paced house beat poured out of the speakers.

"Looks like you better find your seat." Ryder sat down, relief making her lightheaded when Devin followed her lead—for once. "Are you on the front row, too?"

Nigel peered down his generous nose at her. "No. I prefer to have a more realistic experience with the actual consumers."

"Of course you do." She used the same voice as when her Newfoundland, Kermit, became convinced he was a lap dog.

The insult wasn't lost on Nigel, who bared his teeth in an antagonistic imitation of a smile. "It was so nice to meet you…Ryder, wasn't it? Just be sure not to let him drive. It's safer that way."

The bastard melted into the crowd hustling to find their seats.

Devin's profile had turned to stone, except for the throbbing vein at his temple and the twitch in his left eye that had gone into overdrive. Guilt? Or resentment over being wrongly persecuted? He hadn't denied Nigel's accusations. Either way, she'd get to the truth.

But first, they still had to track down Sarah Molina.

• • •

Devin curled his fingers around the Jeep's steering wheel tight enough that his knuckles whitened. For the first time in years, he wasn't sure he could turn the key in the ignition. The remembered smells of burned rubber and Jack Daniels practically hovered in the air, mixing with the real life island scents rolling in on the waves. The engine's roar might just take him all the way back to that night, and he couldn't go back there.

Not when so much was on the line.

Clenching his jaw, he grasped the key already in the

ignition and turned it. The rental's engine sputtered to life.

Ryder yanked open the Jeep's passenger door and slid in, her tablet in her hands. "Okay, I downloaded a live satellite feed of Sarah's family farm to go with the map of it we already have. I'll navigate, you drive. It's at the heart of the island in the De Mis Promesas volcano's shadow. Take the main highway and then a dirt road to the farmstead. It should take about thirty minutes to get there."

Devin made it to the turnoff in twenty, barely noticing the lush green fields of island grass on either side of the road or the volcano getting bigger in the windshield with every mile.

"So, are you going to explain what happened back there?" Ryder's face remained relaxed, but a hard edge sharpened her tone.

He shifted in his seat and slid his gaze away from her. "What do you mean?"

"Don't give me that shit." She slapped her hand against the dashboard. "We're stuck together until we get Sarah back, and I need to know what that Nigel guy was talking about."

Everyone always wanted to know about that night. His father. The police. His so-called friends. The lawyers. Even George had asked him about it one night after the old man had had three too many. Even after a decade, Devin could recite the whole horrific episode by rote with cold, clinical detachment—on the outside. Inside, he heard the screech of tires, the girl's scream, and the squelch of his brother fighting to fill his lungs. It never went away.

The steering wheel bit into his palms. "Why didn't you just try to look it up yourself? You're the investigator."

"I did." She turned in her seat toward him, slipped off her heels, and yanked on a pair of tennis shoes she'd tossed in the Jeep earlier that morning. "Your file is so clean it's like you're a ghost. You don't even have a record of a traffic ticket."

No doubt he had his father to thank for that little gift. If you couldn't use the connections being a billionaire offered to hush up your son's transgressions—even the loser son who'd always disappointed you—what was the point of having all that money?

"Well, then." Bitterness lay thick in his words. "Guess that should tell you something."

"Such as?"

"That it's none of your damn business." Turning off the main road, he pulled in behind a small copse of trees and shifted the Jeep into park. He focused on the single-story house in the distance even as Ryder's nearness called out to him. "We have a job to do. Let's just do it and get the hell off this island."

# Chapter Ten

*"Never in the history of fashion has so little material been raised so high to reveal so much that needs to be covered so badly."*

— *Cecil Beaton*

Pineapple plants dotted the flat ground between Ryder and the Molina farm house. Each pineapple sat in the middle of a four-foot high spiky bush with longer versions of the hard leaves on the top of the pineapple jutting out from all sides. The house itself was a simple, one-story structure on two-foot high stilts. A white tent, large enough for a fifty-person reception, was staked to the ground in front of the house. The sun glinted off of wine bottles and champagne glasses scattered around the wraparound porch.

"Looks like the cleaning crew hasn't arrived yet," she muttered.

Birds swooped across the sky in large looping arcs, their

wide wings a dark shadow in the clear blue sky. A breeze with only a hint of salty ocean brushed against the damp nape of Ryder's neck as she squatted beside Devin behind a three-feet-high rock wall.

Her sixth sense promised they weren't alone with the pineapples, yet not a soul moved in the yard. "Where is everyone?"

"Still sleeping it off from the party?" Devin handed her back the small binoculars she'd stuffed in her purse before they left the hotel that morning.

"No way. This is a working farm. Look at the pineapples. They're lined up perfectly and there's not a stray bit of green anywhere." She scanned the perimeter. There wasn't so much as a curtain flutter in the window. "The question becomes, is Sarah home and waiting to spring a trap, or are we five minutes behind her yet again?"

"How do you propose we figure out which one it is?"

"Easy." Ryder shrugged. "I'll get a closer look."

His fingers wrapped around her wrist, holding her in position. "*We'll* get a closer look."

Her skin burned under his touch and her heartbeat ticked a faster beat, sending a flush of warmth up her chest. "Really? Do we have to do this right now?"

"Yes."

Yanking her hand away, she rubbed her wrist, the tingles dancing across her skin having nothing to do with pain or annoyance, which pissed her off even more. It was a wholly unwelcome reaction to being anywhere near Devin. She hated admitting he was right about anything, but he was on the money about one thing. They had to get off this island. If they didn't, they'd just end up fighting or fucking again and, dammit all, she wasn't sure which one of the two would be worse.

But sitting on her ass watching the pineapples grow sure

as hell wasn't helping her figure that last bit out.

"Fine, let's go." She vaulted over the wall and hustled down the hill, sticking close to the trees for coverage.

They cleared the pineapple field in under a minute, coming to a stop behind a whitewashed shed. She pressed her back against an outbuilding, her shirt snagging on the dried out and cracking wood. There was barely enough room for her and Devin to stand with their shoulders touching, but without any limbs peeking out from the building's sides. Blood rushing in her ears, she craned her neck to take a quick look around the corner. Two hundred feet of dirt crisscrossed with tire tracks from at least five vehicles stood between her and the house, but no vehicles were there.

Her lips flattened and her nails bit into her palms. What she wouldn't give to crack a teapot over Sarah's head right about now. With practiced effort, she pushed the urge to lash out from her mind. Revenge gave a buzz for sure, but getting the job done was a high that lasted longer.

After rolling her head from side to side, she shook out her arms to relieve the tension building within her muscles. Breaking the crockery wasn't going to do a damn thing to fix this cluster fuck. To do that, she needed to get the bitch on the Dylan's Department Store jet.

She straightened so the outbuilding once again hid her from view. A plan started to gel in her mind. "I'm gonna sneak up to the side of the house. You stay here and watch my back."

"No fucking way."

"Look. I'm faster than you are, and I make a smaller target."

"And I can be a more effective backup when I'm right next to you than when I'm two-thirds of a football field away." He pulled her close, his face only inches from hers. "You know you don't always have to prove what a back-in-black total badass you are."

She stumbled back, pulling out of his grasp. That hit too close to home for her to react any way but defensively. "Have you ever not been in total control?"

His face went dark. "Yeah, and it ended up with a kid dead." He rubbed his palm against his close-cropped hair as if he could scrub away what must be an unpleasant memory. "I'm coming with you."

Something about the way he made his declaration shivered its way up her spine. There were moments in the ring when she had to make a split-second decision based on nothing more than training and her gut feeling. This was one of those moments.

"Just don't fuck this up." Without waiting for his reply, she took off at a jog around the outbuilding.

Her tennis shoes thumped across the hard-packed dirt driveway. With her gaze flicking from the house to the pineapple field to the line of trees behind her destination, she listened for any sound. Only Devin's surprisingly light steps behind her pierced the thunder of her heartbeat.

Avoiding the front window, she ran to the side of the house. Devin stopped next to her a second later. She held a finger to her lips then jerked her chin at the first of three windows. He pointed at himself. Nodding, she soft-pedaled it to the second window. Pressing her fingers lightly against the scarred wood, she stood on her tiptoes and peeked inside.

After blinking rapidly to adjust her eyes to the dimmer interior, she squinted and tried to decipher what she was seeing. Floral wallpaper in the kind of pastels that her sister, Alessandra, loved. A white porcelain claw-foot tub. Stacks of petal-pink towels.

She sank back on her heels, turned to Devin, and mouthed the word "bathroom." He nodded, pointed up, and mouthed "kitchen." In tandem, they approached the third window. A *thunk* sounded and a woman yelled in Spanish. Sarah Molina.

The name ran through Ryder's mind, calming the mad beating of her heart.

Adrenaline numbing any bit of healthy fear, she stood so she was eye level with the window. The yelling continued, but the only thing she could pick out in the interior's soft glow was a cat sitting on the arm of a rose-colored couch. The cat lifted a paw, shifting in the process, and the woman's yelling was replaced by a man singing. The corner of a black remote stuck out from under the cat's fuzzy butt.

Ryder's Call of Duty kick-ass mentality fizzled into a grin at the sight.

"Everyone hates missing their favorite shows," Devin whispered.

She choked back a giggle as her pulse returned to normal. "You should have seen my Nonni when they moved Judge Judy's time slot. Sicilians are serious about their curses."

"I'll keep that in mind."

The crunch of many tires killed the light mood.

They scurried to the corner and peered around.

A series of four trucks pulled up in the dirt driveway, coming to rest next to the house's front porch. Two men climbed out of each vehicle, circled around to unload stacks of boxes from the truck beds, and carried the cargo inside. A minute later, the cat meowed, and the sounds of men talking and laughing filtered out of the window.

Catching Devin's gaze, she pointed up, then toward the trucks. He nodded and pivoted on his haunches so he would be ready if any of the men came around the corner.

She inhaled a deep breath through her nose and exhaled from her mouth before rising. Five men were in the living room. The oldest one, who must have been in his late fifties, lifted the flaps of one of the boxes and pulled out a teapot.

*So much for the Sopranos of The Andol Republic.*

Then he pulled off the kettle's lid and reached inside.

What he retrieved put rainbows on the walls. Focusing her attention on his hands, she tried to make out what he held. No luck—until he lifted the object for the rest of the crew to admire. A diamond choker dangled from his fingers.

*Shit.*

Ryder sank down below the sill. "We've gotta get to the cops," she whispered.

"Drugs?"

She shook her head. "Stolen diamonds."

"*Huh?*"

Before she could answer, a furry flash appeared as the cat leaped out and sailed over their heads. A second later, a man stuck his head out and hollered at the feline.

*Double shit.*

He glanced down and his lips formed a smile that would have made the devil hesitate. "*Hola, Americanos.*"

Acting on instinct, Ryder reached up, curled her fingers around the man's shirt front, and tugged. He tumbled out of the window and landed with an audible *umph* at her feet. He popped up and yelled for his compatriots just before her fist connected with his windpipe. The man's eyes bulged and he dropped to his knees like an anchor tossed overboard. He flopped over to his side, knocking his head on a rock. Lights out.

"Nice job." Devin nudged her and pointed to the window. "But there's more work ahead."

She whipped around. Two muscular men were staring at them from the other side of the window. Footsteps thundered through the house. A screen door creaked, then smacked against the siding. At the same time, the two guys leaped over the paint-cracked window frame.

As if they'd been doing it their whole lives, she and Devin instantly took positions back to back, guards up and fists ready.

"You take care of the assholes in the window." A feral grin transformed Devin's face as a group of men rounded the corner. "I got these five."

"Don't worry." Using her thumb, she cracked each knuckle on her right hand, her eyes never leaving the duo in front of her. "I'll be done with these two in plenty of time to help you clean up."

Both men stood an inch or two shorter than her. But what they lacked in height, they more than made up for in bulk. The one with shoulder-length hair looked her up and down, his leering gaze never going higher than her tits or lower than her hips. Laughing, Long Hair nudged his freckle-faced buddy and let out a stream of fast-clipped Spanish as they stood shoulder-to-shoulder in front of her.

Ryder only recognized one word: *puta*.

She could do bitch. Hell, it would be rude to disappoint them. Raising her fists to protect her face, she rolled her weight to the balls of her feet then blew the ring leader a kiss.

Long Hair sauntered forward, smirking at her and leaving all the vulnerable spots north of his collarbone unprotected. That was a mistake. A big one.

She winked at him…just before landing an uppercut to his chin that snapped his head back like a rubber band. He stumbled back, but she wasn't about to give him a chance to get his bearings. Her second punch connected with his left eye, which she followed with a high kick to the side of his head.

Wrapping her arm around Long Hair's neck in a choke hold, she pivoted just in time to use him as a shield against Freckles's punch. The hit landed square in Long Hair's solar plexus. The punch rattled her teeth, so she wasn't surprised when Long Hair's knees gave way and he turned into a wet noodle in her arms. She shoved him forward into Freckles. Both men staggered back before Freckles shoved Limp Hair face-first into the dirt, sending up a small brown cloud.

The element of surprise gone, she had to take a different approach to neutralize Freckles. They circled each other, both ignoring the fight behind them as Devin took on the rest of the Molina's thugs. Ryder took advantage of the slowdown in the action to bring her breathing under control and assessed her new opponent. She had an easy two inches on him, giving her the wing—and leg—span advantage, but all the pale brown spots covering the creep's face didn't mask the jagged knife scar on his left cheekbone or the tear tattoos under his right eye. Long Hair might be the leader, but the air around Freckles vibrated with evil intent.

All the lessons she'd learned while sparring with Cam at Paulie's Gym came into perfect focus. *Keep your guards up. Don't stop moving. Attack first. Hit hard and hit often. Aim to disable. Then get the fuck out.*

The *whump* of a body hitting a hard object sounded by the corner of the house, followed by a moan of agony. Freckles's gaze flicked to the side for a split second. Long enough for her to get off two solid punches to his face. He retaliated with a solid jab to her sternum. Pain exploded in her chest and her defenses faltered. Seizing the advantage, he backhanded her across the face hard enough that her ears rang and she lost her balance, landing hard on her side. Pebbles hidden in the dirt bit into her cheek.

Alarms screamed in her head. Paulie's mantra echoed in her head. *No one wins from the floor.* She had to get up now or she'd be dead. A shadow appeared and she rolled, narrowly missing the strike of a steel-toed boot aimed at her skull. Clawing up a handful of earth, she scrambled up and tossed it into Freckles's face.

He howled and wiped the brown muck from his eyes.

Ryder kneed him in the balls, remembering to hit him as if she could kick straight through him. He cried out and doubled over. Hitting him where it counted would slow him down, but it wouldn't take him out, so she cocked her arm and struck him directly in the nose, aiming upward. A crack sounded and blood spurted everywhere. A roundhouse kick finished him off.

Lungs heaving, she turned to find Devin facing off against two men going at him at the same time. Two others lay on the ground. A third stood off to the side, his attention wholly focused on the two-on-one. Another mistake.

Reacting on pure animal instinct, she sped toward the action, stooping low to swipe up a baseball bat-length tree limb from the ground. She had it cocked and aimed at the dickweed's head before he even realized she was there. The violence of the impact ricocheted up her arms. He crumbled to the ground.

Devin landed a hard haymaker to one opponent's right eye. His elbow connected with the second guy's solar plexus. What followed was a vicious combination of hits and kicks to both men. The whole thing looked more like a caged mixed martial arts fight than a street fight. He might work in fashion, but the muscles and ink weren't just for show—dollars to donuts, he'd earned both the old-fashioned way. Within thirty seconds, he had the men moaning on the ground.

"Let's get the fuck out of here before more show up," she called to him.

He nodded and sprinted to the front porch, grabbed an empty wine bottle, and smashed it against the railing. Dark red liquid splashed over the wood. Gripping the bottle neck, he trotted down the steps to the driveway and plunged the sharp edge into the trucks' tires, flattening at least one tire on each of the four trucks.

Then they took off across the pineapple field, dodging the spiky bushes as they made quick work of the distance. They had to get to the police before the rest of the Molina family found them.

• • •

The local police headquarters was housed in the only two-story building on the island. The tan stone structure stood like a plain cousin amongst the brightly colored stores that lined Andol City's downtown. And because this whole trip was FUBARed already, it seemed appropriate that the station sat right across the street from Tea Time.

Ryder would give the Molinas one thing, they had balls. It took big stones to locate a smuggling cover operation dead in the local authorities'ysights. That either meant they were overly cocky or legitimately confident in their ability to get away with their crimes. Considering how the islanders reacted with either fear or guilt whenever she brought up the Molinas, it was probably the latter. Dirty cops were a reality all over the world. Still, as a cop's kid, not notifying the police about a crime was akin to growing up with dentists for parents and never brushing your teeth.

She twisted in her seat to give Devin her full attention. "There's a good chance the cops are on the family payroll."

"Agreed." He nodded. "Which is why this is a stupid move."

She clenched her teeth and made it to five before exploding. When it came to her personal life her instincts were for shit, but when it mattered—when lives were on the line—her gut was good. "You're not in charge of this investigation. I am. And I say we're going to the cops."

"Why?" He hurled the question at her like a hand grenade.

"Because shit is hitting the fan and I don't like our odds. We won't know for sure if the cops are bought until we get in there. We can't assume. That's how people get hurt." Flames beat against her cheeks and she had to stop and take a deep breath. Calmer, she continued. "Keep everything close to the vest until we figure it out."

Though he clearly didn't like it, he grunted his assent and circled around to the back of the station, where he parked the Jeep in the lot bordering the alley. That would keep the hot pink vehicle out of sight from Dominga, who no doubt was on the lookout from her perch at the tea shop.

Devin turned off the motor. "You ready?"

Ryder glanced in the Jeep's visor mirror at the bruises forming on the left side of her face and winced. "Why is it that cuts and bruises always hurt more once you actually see them?"

"Because life is a real bitch that way." He wiped his thumb across the corner of his mouth, clearing away some of the dried blood, but a new trickle started as soon as he removed pressure. "Let's get this winning plan over with."

No longer bathed in pain-blocking adrenaline, her body ached as they crossed the parking lot. Without even looking, she figured she could pinpoint at least fifteen bruises from her toes to her eyebrows. No broken bones, thank God, but enough hurt to slow her step and add a slight limp to compensate for a pain in her right thigh.

Devin wasn't quite at his normal pace, either. Pea green bruises covered his swollen jaw. His left eye had puffed out, foretelling of a hell of a shiner tomorrow. What other injuries lay hidden under his white linen shirt and dark slacks, she could only guess at based on his deliberate pace and the way he held his right arm away from his side.

"Your ribs broken?" Ryder grabbed the handle of the glass door and pulled it open.

He shook his head. "Bruised. I'll live."

An overhead fan pushed stale, humid air around the barren front lobby. It was "decorated" by a few folding chairs, an empty desk, and large, full color portraits of The Andol Republic's president and vice president. An older model computer monitor took up a third of the space on the desk, an empty wire in-and-out basket sat on the opposite side, and a hotel bell sat in the middle. A small folded note in front of the bell read: *Receptionist at lunch. Ring for service.*

She did. Nothing happened.

"Anyone home?" Devin's voice boomed in the quiet room.

"I'll be with you in one moment," a voice called from the hallway to the right.

A second later, an officer wearing a light blue uniform shirt and tan khaki pants appeared in a wheelchair at the end of the hall. He rolled toward them. "Sorry about that, I just returned from lunch and the other officers on duty just left for theirs." He stopped behind the desk. "*Dios*, what happened to you two? Shall I call for medical attention?"

"No, thank you." Devin paused and looked at Ryder. "Unless you need it?"

Ryder shook her head. "No. Just banged up."

The officer looked skeptical but let the idea of a hospital slide. "So how about you start at the beginning and walk me through what happened." He pulled several sheets of paper from a desk drawer and retrieved a pen from a cup holder. "Let's start with your names."

She and Devin took turns explaining they were in The Andol Republic for the fashion week events, being sure to leave out that the old friend they were looking for had embezzled almost five million dollars, as well as exactly how they'd ended up at Sarah's pineapple farm. The longer they told their story, the more the officer clammed up, and the more often he looked behind him as if waiting for the boogeyman to attack.

Ryder's skin crawled. The officer might not be dirty but,

judging by his nervous ticks, he wouldn't going to be any help, either.

"And you just accidentally ended up at the Molina family farm…where thugs attacked you for no apparent reason?" the officer asked, a noticeable shake bouncing each syllable before it left his lips.

Telling him about the diamonds wasn't going to do anything but give any dirty cops and the Molinas more motivation to hunt them down. As far as the Molinas knew now, she and Devin had never seen the stolen jewelry.

"That's right," she answered as she shot Devin a telling glance that she hoped yelled *keep your mouth shut*.

"They jumped us for no reason at all," Devin all but growled.

The officer gulped and took a slow look around the nearly empty room, his eyes settling on the closed entry door before returning to them.

Ryder's stomach twisted. Whatever was coming next, she wasn't going to like.

"I once filed a report very similar to this one." The officer faltered, but only for a moment, then an unconvincing smile appeared on his face. "I've been in this wheelchair ever since." He raised a hand. "Not that I'm saying you shouldn't make your report. Just know there are consequences on this island for this type of action—even for a policeman. For a tourist whom no one here knows or will miss…"

Forget about having elephant *cajones* to establish a crime business front across from the police station. The Molina family obviously didn't waste time worrying about the cops. If they could do whatever it took to put a cop in a wheelchair, they feared nothing.

"Thank God you weren't more seriously injured by these…unknown hooligans,"othe officer said.

Devin crossed his arms, the motion making him grimace.

"Are you going to investigate this at all?"

"Of course, but we are a small department." The officer shrugged. "It may take some time before our detective can look into your allegations."

Ryder couldn't believe the Molina assholes were going to get away with it all, and probably not for the first time. But it looked like that was exactly what would happen—unless she and Devin did something about it. "I see."

"I hope you do," the cop murmured.

Devin pushed up from his chair and headed for the door. Ryder followed suit. A police cruiser pulled into the parking lot as they pulled out. The two officers inside gave the Jeep a long, hard stare before one of the cops winked. His smile was anything but friendly.

Obviously, there wasn't much else she and Devin could accomplish through official channels. Whatever happened next, it was up to them.

# Chapter Eleven

*"I think it's the responsibility of a designer to try to break rules and barriers."*

— *Gianni Versace*

Fifteen minutes later, Devin's silent treatment was about to make Ryder nuts. If it wasn't for the birds chirping, there wouldn't have been a sound inside the vehicle as he steered the Jeep down the same highway the Palm Inn was located on. Frustrated aggression rolled off him in swells big enough to flatten her curly hair into stick-straight strands.

Well, he wasn't the only one pissed off at the world right now. Staying quiet after the crap sandwich they'd just been served had her twitchy, but despite her attempts to get a conversation going, Devin had completely ignored her— unless you counted him double-checking her safety belt, which she did not. At the pineapple farm, they'd clicked as if they'd been working together for years. No second thoughts.

No second guessing. Everything right the first time. Now the pendulum had swung back to fractious, and it pissed Ryder off more than she wanted to admit. The inability to run away from or punch the annoyance had her as edgy as her dog during a thunderstorm.

Keeping her focus on the sidewalks and buildings they passed, watching for signs of trouble, she decided to give it one more shot before the tension ate a hole through her stomach lining.

"Where are we going?" Walking away from a half dozen black tank tops and a few pairs of jeans wasn't going to kill her. However, finding members of the Molina family or the winking cop in her room just might. "We can't go back to the hotel."

"Agreed."

One syllable was an improvement compared to silencer mode, but she was going to strangle him with her shoelaces if he didn't form a full sentence soon. "So, are you going to tell me, or do I need to finish the job those goons started?"

He suddenly grinned, and it was 100 percent pure, cocky, testosterone-driven jock. "You really think you can take me?"

"Without a doubt." *Okay, maybe a little doubt.*

His fingers relaxed against the steering wheel. "How about once we get back to Harbor City, I give you a chance?"

"Challenge accepted." In reality, home was a world away, but at the moment, it felt like it was in another solar system. "Now spill, where are you driving us?"

"I found a tent and camping supplies in the back of the Jeep yesterday when I grabbed our bags. Must be included in the rental. We can camp in the nature preserve outside of town."

Not surprisingly, the idea of roughing it seemed more appealing than it had the other day. The Molina family had located them at the Palm Inn despite the fact that they'd registered as Mr. and Mrs. Fitzsimmons. Even if they could find a room in another hotel, which was doubtful, it wouldn't be long before Sarah's family knew exactly where they were. And this time they wouldn't stop at taking incriminating photos of her and Devin getting down and dirty.

While he drove, she grabbed her tablet from the glove compartment, pulled up the Maltese Security encrypted messaging system, and began typing.

CARLOS, I NEED A GPS TRACK PUT ON SARAH MOLINA'S CELL. THE NUMBER'S IN THE FILE.

She hit enter and waited. If she knew their tech guru, he'd be glued to a screen somewhere. A notification beeped a few seconds later.

CONSIDER IT DONE.

Ryder laid the tablet in her lap. "Carlos is putting a track on Sarah's cell phone. That'll give us her coordinates, as long as she hasn't disabled the GPS or turned off her phone."

"It'll be on in the morning." Devin sounded sure.

Ryder hiked a brow. "What makes you say that?"

"Her mother is in an assisted living center in Harbor City. She calls her every morning at nine sharp. Everyone on the executive level at Dylan's Department Store knew better than to buzz George's office between nine and nine-thirty."

Finally a break. Even with her family connections, Sarah wouldn't be able to hide out on the tiny island much longer. "I'll let 'Los know." Ryder's thumbs flew across the screen as she texted the update to Carlos. "We only have forty-eight hours until George has to open the books to MultiCorp."

"We'll find her." His firm tone didn't leave room for doubt.

She peeked at him from the corner of her eye. His right cheekbone had turned the same shade of purple as a fresh eggplant. "I hope there's a first aid kit in the back, because you're going to need some ice packs tonight."

He cracked a smile with only the smallest of grimaces.

"You're not looking so hot yourself, sweetheart."

Her responding wry chuckle caught on the island breeze as they passed the hotel and continued west, heading toward the coast. She didn't even have to glance in the rearview mirror to know he was right. She snickered softly. Sylvie and Drea were always on her to wear more color…but she highly doubted this was what they had in mind.

Devin pulled off the highway at the sign for the Andol Nature Preserve. The road was a lot bumpier than the highway, jostling her as she fought to hold herself still so her protesting muscles wouldn't scream as loud. They passed hikers weighed down with backpacks and reusable water bottles who were heading deeper inland. Pop-up tents in various shades of blue dotted the landscape like blueberries in a muffin.

"The preserve is a popular spot," Devin said. "No better place to hide than in plain sight."

"Good plan."

"Wait, you're not biting my head off for making an executive decision?" He shifted into a lower gear as the road hit a five percent incline. "Did that guy whack you in the head or something?"

"Very funny." She rolled her eyes.

About five miles down the road, an outcropping of trees appeared on the right. A few miles later, one of the island's ubiquitous rock walls ran along the left side of the road, a few yards in.

Devin pulled off and parked the Jeep behind the wall. "Figured we could hump it back to the trees to spend the night. They're looking for a hot pink Jeep, not a small tent."

"It's not my idea of fun, but it's better than dealing with the Molinas' muscle before we get a chance to patch ourselves up."

Before she could grab any of the supplies out of the back, Devin had gathered them. He had so many bags he looked like a pack mule walking on its hind legs.

She sidled up to him. "Give me some of that."

"No. You're banged up."

"Like you're not." She held out her hand. "Give."

With great reluctance, he handed over the sleeping bag and the first aid kit, keeping the tent and assorted gear for himself. Rolling her eyes, she turned and headed back toward the trees. Walking down the road as the first stars appeared wasn't the best of options, but it sure as hell beat walking in the high grass and leaving a trail of bent greenery straight to their campsite.

Thankfully, the small pop-up tent assembled with a minimum of fuss, and within fifteen minutes, they were inside tending to their wounds.

Using the chrome camping coffee pot as a mirror, she swiped her face with a sterile wipe before dabbing antiseptic on the scrapes. The bruise looked a garish purple reflected in the funhouse mirror of the metal, but she doubted it would look any better in a real mirror.

Devin groaned behind her as he tried to pull his shirt over his head instead of unbuttoning it all the way.

"Here, let me help." She shuffled over on her knees.

He brushed her away. "I can manage."

He lifted his arms again and his face lost a shade or two of color.

"Not so much, Mr. Tough Guy. You can't even get your shirt off. Now shut up and let me help."

She undid his buttons as he sat cross legged, the light from the propane lantern glinting off her gold rope bracelet, and pushed the linen material away from his chest. Puce yellow, pea green, and a funky shade of darkest blue clashed with the tattoo panorama across his muscular midsection. She traced her fingers down his ribs. He'd promised her nothing was broken, but she wouldn't put it past him to lie about it.

Three-fourths of the way down the gnarly bruise, he grabbed her hand. "I'm fine."

She cracked a rapid-cold pack and held it to the bruise. "Did you get the license plate of the Mack truck that hit you?"

"You're such a comedian." He turned away and rubbed the back of his head, revealing a patchwork of angry red slashes across his back and rough-looking gashes where his knuckles had connected with the thugs' hard bones. "You can have the sleeping bag, I'll just—"

"Not so fast." She gripped his forearm and the skin-to-skin contact sent a jolt of electricity straight to her core. "You've got cuts and scrapes all over you."

She ignored his grumbling and started with his knuckles before moving on to his face, smoothing her hands over his five o'clock shadow and feeling for tenderness. His skin heated beneath her touch and the pulse in his neck jumped. By the time she was caring for the one-inch cut on his cheekbone, the ache in her hip had been replaced by one between her thighs. God, she'd make the world's worst Florence Nightingale, if she kept getting all worked up while dotting a guy's face with Neosporin.

Her sanity couldn't take much more, so she started to hum an old song her mom used to sing to her whenever she'd woken up with a nightmare. Devin jerked under her touch.

"I'm sorry, did I hurt you?"

"No." None of the light, teasing tone from earlier remained. Instead, his deep voice sounded hollow. "It's the song."

Something in the aching emptiness of his tone pulled at Ryder. "You know it?"

"It was my brother's favorite when he was a little kid. He used to sing it every day just to drive me nuts." His voice broke. "Now he can't even remember the name of it."

She digested that for a few moments, hurting for Devin.

"What happened?" she asked softly.

"I failed at the most important job every big brother has—to protect your younger siblings. I almost killed him." He paused. "I wonder sometimes if it wouldn't be better if I had. James was one of those fifteen year-olds you read about who are already going to college. He was halfway through earning his BA in physics when he came home to visit."

Devin stared out at the starry sky through the circular mesh window in the roof of the tent, but the darkness in his eyes extinguished the starlight that should have been reflected there.

"A bunch of us used to drive down to Waterburg to drag race the locals. It was a great way for stupid twenty-somethings with too much time and money on their hands to blow off steam. James had never been, so it seemed like the perfect brother-bonding time when he came home for spring break, plus it got him away from Dad, who was always pressuring him not to take a minute away from school. Most of the time, the police would break it up before we'd been there for long, but not always. When the cops arrived that night, it was too late. My cherry red BMW roadster was overturned off the side of the road, with my brother and me hanging upside down. The car I was racing against, a Mustang, had gone head-to-head with a tree and lost. Badly."

The back of Ryder's throat tightened and she reached for a strand of hair. But this time the smooth feel of it wrapping around her fingers as she twisted did little to alleviate the anxiety churning her insides into mush.

Devin white-knuckled the steering wheel and went on, "I crawled out of the Beemer with a few superficial scratches. The kid in the other car wasn't as lucky. He'd gone straight through his windshield and died in the ambulance on the way to the hospital."

Ryder actually remembered the accident. The kid who

died was from their neighborhood. Richie Vivier. He'd been a few years ahead of her in school. She hadn't known him well, but he'd been on the football team with her brother, Tony. The night of the accident, their father had come home after working the scene, hugged all of the kids, and locked himself in the den for the night. He'd played Otis Redding and gotten stone-cold drunk.

"There was an investigation, but no charges were ever filed," Devin said, each word more painful to hear than the last. "The other driver's family filed a civil complaint but dropped it a few months after they received an anonymous cash donation. My dad paid half a million dollars to hush the whole thing up."

Ryder blinked. Jesus.

"One kid died, I walked away with scratches, but only a shadow version of James got out of that car." His voice wavered on the last word but he took a deep breath and continued. "He suffered permanent brain damage and lives in a resident care facility. He had a genius level IQ and now he has no fucking clue how to work a TV remote control. I did that to him. It was my fault."

A bone-deep ache for him wracked Ryder. She wanted to reach out, to comfort him, but Devin was clearly a man barely hanging on. She'd grown up in a family of cops, tough men who refused to admit their own pain or wanted others acknowledging it. Touching Devin might be just the thing that would push him over the edge, so she curled her fingers around the gold blessing bracelet that matched his.

"I killed one kid and ruined another." Devin's voice strengthened, but beneath the volume lay an ocean of pain. "And yeah, I walked away with only a couple of bruises, but there's not a day when I don't pay for it. Not a single fucking day. But obviously I'm too stupid to have learned my lesson. I should have been watching out for you today. There's no way in hell I should have let you go gladiator against two thugs. I almost got you killed today and that is not acceptable."

• • •

Devin's throat closed around a lump of blame and regret he could never fully banish. Raw and angry, he wanted to fight back against the disappointment and shame, but he couldn't drown it in alcohol or beat it away with a punching bag. God knew he'd tried both already. The guilt always returned every time he cracked open his eyelids with the morning sun.

"Today was *not* your fault, Devin. You didn't lead me into anything. It was *my* plan. And if you recall, I ran in front of you, not behind you. Anyway, I would have liked to have seen you try to stop me." The pity in her dark brown eyes nearly undid him.

*My fault. Again.*

How many people did he have to hurt before he accepted that his father had been right? He was a dumb jock who reacted first and thought second. Sure, he'd moved up the corporate ladder, but he couldn't ever shake the idea that the whole thing was a fluke. After college, he'd devoted five years to MMA training. Maybe he should have continued. At least then the people he hurt would have signed up for it. God knew he had. His opponents' fists had been punishing, but never as bad as he deserved. His mission whenever he'd entered the ring had never been to win. It had been to have his opponent knock the memories from his head.

If only it had worked.

He brushed his fingers over the green bruises slashing across Ryder's cheek, guilt burning through him. "You were hurt."

"Yeah, that happens. I'll be fine in a few days. I'm tougher than I look. She lifted the antiseptic cloth to the cut at the corner of his mouth. "This is gonna hurt like a mother."

She screwed up her face, twisting her lips and flaring her nostrils like her skin was made of Silly Putty. The goofy action broke the tension and he laughed, clearing away the darkness fogging his thoughts.

How she managed to shake the ground beneath him, he couldn't understand. But she did. And it scared him more than the biggest, baddest fighter he'd ever stared down.

"I'm tougher than I look, too," he assured her.

She sat back and cocked her head, giving him a playful up and down appraisal. "I don't know how that's possible, you look like a total badass."

"Don't all carnival kissing booth champions?" He waggled his eyebrows, making her giggle.

The cloth stung when she pressed it to his skin, but only for a moment. Seeing the way she sucked on her bottom lip as she contemplated treating his other bruises distracted him from the pain. Ryder was beautiful and sexy, but that wasn't why she'd haunted him since their first night together.

That night should have been a few hours of anonymous sex, a simple release between two consenting adults. But he couldn't deny what he'd known on an instinctual level the moment he'd rolled over that morning and found her side of the bed empty.

They fit.

That explained the follow-up calls he'd made and why her rebuff had made him react like a wounded bear, snarling and swiping at her every chance he got. The epiphany crashed against his thick skull so hard he couldn't deny it any longer. She challenged him, pushed every one of his buttons, and egged him on with her accept-no-bullshit attitude.

When he was with her, he didn't want to be a better man. He already was.

Her gaze caught his and in a heartbeat, the teasing look in

them faded, overpowered by the hunger that must have been reflected in his own.

The cloth slipped from her grasp, a white flash in his periphery vision.

Neither of them moved. It was as if the earth stopped circling the sun and the moon let loose its hold on the tides. In one breath, anything could happen. Whether she leaned in or he moved toward her, he couldn't tell. All he knew was that in the next second his lips were on hers. She tasted of honey lip balm, mangoes, and endless possibilities.

God, she took his breath away.

# Chapter Twelve

*"Fashion is all about eventually becoming naked."*

*— Rene Konig*

Amazed and in awe, Devin held his breath as his fingertips grazed Ryder's silky smooth skin, soft as hummingbird's wings. His touch slipped down her throat as she arched her head back, drawing him deeper into the kiss, surrendering and demanding at the same time as only she did. Soft and hard. Giving and taking. Everywhere and nowhere. Intoxicated on the conflicting combinations that made up Ryder, he tugged the band holding her hair in place until her long waves fell down her back. He weaved his fingers through the lush, dark-chocolate strands, letting the glossy river pour through his hands.

She pulled back, bracing a palm gently against his shoulder, concern and desire warring in her dark eyes. "Your ribs."

"Are fine." In truth, his ribs hurt like a bitch, but he'd dealt with more pain for a whole lot less pleasure than being with Ryder. Touching her was worth a hell of a lot more severe injuries than a few bruised ribs. Hooking his fingers into her belt loops, he tugged her down until her knees were on either side of his hips.

"But you're — "

Devin cut off her unneeded concern by sliding his hands up her thighs, the pads of his thumbs following the seam of her pants, stopping just short of the juncture of her thighs. So fucking close to the promised land, yet so far away. Desperate to feel her, he stroked the center seam where it nestled against her heated center.

"Devin — " She sucked in a sharp breath and scraped her teeth against her cherry-stained bottom lip.

"A few aches are nothing compared to how badly I want to be inside you right now." He trailed his lips down her throat, nipping her sensitive flesh as he slid his hands around to her ass. Squeezing the round flesh through her pants, he slid her forward until she rocked against his hard cock. Her heat seeped through the material separating them and he had to fight the caveman impulse to rip her clothes off and sink himself into her depths in one long stroke.

She hesitated, considering him with a heavy-lidded gaze as his heart hammered against his bruised ribs. Then she dropped her fingers to the tiny onyx-colored buttons on her shirt.

This time it was his breath that caught as she revealed inch after inch of olive-toned skin.

With each button she slipped open, Devin's cock hardened, until he worried he would come in his pants just from seeing a few inches of soft skin. Anticipation vibrated up from his balls, hot, demanding, and unwilling to be denied. In the past, he'd always enjoyed a good strip tease, but if Ryder didn't get naked soon, he wasn't sure he'd make it without exploding.

Her eyes alight with seduction, she feathered her fingertips down the length of her open shirt, the edges of which had snagged on the hard tips of her dusky rose-colored nipples. Sucking on her bottom lip, she slid her thumb over the flimsy black fabric and circled the hard peaks while swaying against his rock hard dick. The damp heat of her pussy permeated through the layers between them, taunting him with its closeness. It was the best lap dance he'd ever gotten, and it was going to kill him if she didn't end it soon.

"It's not nice to tease," he said, grinding out the words. "Take off the shirt."

"Always so bossy." She opened it another inch so he could see the edges of her round areolas and held it there for a moment before shrugging it off. The flimsy garment slid down her back and over his hands that were still gripping her perfect ass. Cupping her lush tits in her hands, she pinched her nipples and pulled them taut. "Is this what you wanted?"

"Fuck, yes." He slid his hands upward, spanning her bare back and pulling her close as he flipped them around so she lay naked from the waist up, on the red sleeping bag. Dark purple and green bruises marred the olive skin of her side, where one of the thugs had kicked her. Another darkened the skin near her collarbone.

Rage rushed through him like a runaway train as he reached up to gently touch it. "I'm going to rip their balls off, roast them over a bonfire, and make the assholes eat them like s'mores," he growled.

She licked her full lips and popped open the top button of her pants. "Not right now I hope."

Lust battled with righteous fury, but as she lowered her zipper, revealing a swath ebony silk dotted with emerald-green hearts, he lost the ability to think about anything but her. "God, you're beautiful."

He slipped his palms from her back to curve them around her waist as she lay beneath him, open and vulnerable. He scooted down and dragged his tongue across the stretch of flat skin above her low waistband. He hooked his fingers under the elastic of her panties and tugged the center lower, delivering a kiss to the soft skin above her tight, dark curls.

She shivered underneath him. "Now who's teasing?"

"Turnabout is fair play." He murmured against her heated skin before sitting back and letting her panties snap back in place. "Now let's get these pants off."

"What about you?" Her gaze lowered to the bulge threatening his zipper and she licked her lips as she wriggled out of her pants.

He rolled back onto his heels and rose until he stood crouched over in the tent, and shucked off his slacks and cotton boxers. She sat up, her mouth even with the swollen head of his cock. Keeping her gaze fixed on his face, she wrapped her hands around his girth. His cock jumped at her touch. She grinned and stuck out the tip of her pink tongue, licking her way up the sensitive underside before swiping it across the head, wet with precum.

The temptation to tangle his fingers in her hair and slide his full length into her hot mouth nearly overwhelmed him. But if he did that there was no way he'd last long enough to bury himself inside her, let alone plunge in and out until she squeezed his dick with the power of her orgasm. Only then would he let himself go. He stepped back from her.

"Where are you going? I'm not done yet." She leaned forward and engulfed his length, a hand cupping his balls with one finger extended to stroke the sensitive spot behind his balls.

Pleasure streaked up from the base of his spine and his thighs shook. He surged inside her mouth, her tongue caressing his cock as he moved forward. She hummed against him and he almost nutted on the next breath.

He clamped his jaw together nearly hard enough to crack a tooth and stepped back again. "Enough."

"You don't like?" The wicked upward turn of her delicious lips told him she knew full well just how much he did.

"I like it too much." He pushed her down onto the sleeping bag. "But now it's your turn."

. . .

The slick nylon sleeping bag crinkled under Ryder's back as Devin knelt next to her and slid her panties down her legs. Holding her ankles in his left hand so her feet pointed straight up at the stars peeking through the tent's mesh window, he skimmed his lips down her legs. Setting an achingly slow pace, he licked, kissed, and nipped from her ankles to the back of her knee, setting fire to her skin.

He stroked the back of his fingers down the back of her thighs until his thumb rubbed against the center of her silk panties. "These have got to go."

Ready to rip them in half herself so he would finally touch her aching core, she hooked her fingers into the waist band and, keeping her legs sky-bound, whipped them off. The cool island breeze tickled her damp curls as she spread her legs wide and rested her calves on Devin's broad shoulders.

He growled his approval and traced two fingers around her wet folds. "So ready for me."

Ryder's nails dug into her palms, piercing the fog of desire surrounding her. "Please."

His fingers circled her opening, making her shiver. "Not yet. I want to taste you." He dropped his head between her thighs.

His hot mouth stopped millimeters from her clit, close

enough that she could feel his breath on aching flesh. "Please." She didn't care if she was begging. She needed it. She needed what only he could give her.

"How could I say no to that?" He stroked her clit with his firm tongue before sucking the sensitive nub between his lips. Fire sizzled through her. His teasing fingers circled her wet opening as he continued his mouth's soft assault.

Back arched, her entire body pleaded for more and she rubbed herself against his talented tongue. Answering her call, he increased the pressure. Needing to hold onto something solid so she wouldn't slide off the face of the earth from the intensity of sensation, she twisted the sleeping bag in her hands.

He lifted his face from her center, his mouth wet with the evidence of her desire, and slowed the fingers stroking her opening until it seemed her pussy would implode with want.

Need reverberated through every cell. "Don't stop."

"Don't worry, honey, I'm not stopping anytime soon." He plunged two fingers into her, crossing and uncrossing them as he rubbed her inner walls. His knuckles brushed against her G-spot's tangle of nerves and pleasure ricocheted around her body from the stretch of her arms to the yearning ache in her core.

The combination of pressure and his unhurried pace stole her ability to form words or to think, or to do anything but feel. She twisted her hips against his hand as the vibrations built in her thighs. The tremors in her legs deepened as the tightness in her pussy increased. Everything built higher and tighter, her entire body heaving with need.

Just when she thought she couldn't take anymore, he leaned down and lapped his tongue across her clit, sending her over into the abyss. A strangled moan escaped as her climax poured over her like molten lava. Aftershocks of pleasure reverberated through her as she tried to bring the world back into focus.

Devin raised himself so he lay with his cheek resting on her stomach. His thumbs pressed against her hips and he kissed her belly. "What do you want?"

"You inside me." Need weakened her voice just as it strengthened her determination to have him here and now.

"Why?" He growled the question against the curve of her hip, his fingers anchoring her in place.

Afraid she was going to implode under the pressure of his lips and her lust, she pulled out of his grasp and retreated to the been-there-done-that cynicism that had served her so faithfully. "Because you're a damn good lay. I'm not looking for anything more than a little friendly release."

"Is that the only reason?" He quirked an eyebrow and rolled back up his heels, his hard cock heavy between his legs.

*Yes. No. Maybe.* "You want another one? I'm breaking enough rules already." They were starting to pile up chin high. Was it just a week ago she'd been so set on having a full year of freedom from men and their issues?

He closed the inches between them, a reckless determination darkening his eyes. "I don't think this is the first time you've broken a few rules."

"True." She trailed her fingers up the dragon tattoo on his arm, relishing the twitch of his muscles reacting to her touch and the quickening pace of the vein in his neck. "But you're the one who's making me break them."

"That doesn't change the question." He lowered his head and sucked one of her nipples into his mouth. His tongue swirled once and then twice around the hard tip before he released it. "Why?"

Why *did* she want him inside her so badly? "Because I want to feel something good."

"I hate to break it to you, sugar." He sank a finger between her slick folds and she gasped in his ear. "But I'm pretty fucking far from good."

"Not from where I'm looking." The truth of the statement sank in a moment before his mouth claimed hers. And that's when she knew she was in big trouble.

• • •

Soft, wet, and hot, Ryder melted against Devin, making him harder than he thought possible. She gripped his fingers as he slid them in and out of her, he circled her entrance as she squirmed in his arms. She'd come only moments before and was ready again. His thumb found her clit, rubbing her and pushing against the side of it.

"How about this? Is this good?"

She mumbled something that sounded like, "Yes!" followed by, "Don't fucking stop!"

He rubbed his stubbled cheek against her tits because he knew she liked that and licked the valley between them as the cool night breeze rushed over them. Taking her nipple into his hungry mouth, he teased her with his teeth. Scraping. Tugging. Making her call out his name in a tone that was both plea and promise. It was almost too much.

Almost.

"Got a condom?" he rasped. Refilling his wallet stash hadn't been at the top of his mind since they'd landed.

"Fuck." Ryder rested her head back against the sleeping bag. The frustrated look on her face would have been comical if he hadn't been dealing with the same emotion right then.

"Take me in your hand," he ordered.

Her firm grip encircled him and glided up and down his cock. The world went dark but he managed to continue stroking her and teasing her supple flesh. A flash of gold around her wrist pierced the blackness. Their blessing bracelet. He jiggled his arm so his matching gold rope rolled down to the base of his thumb, then angled his wrist so the bracelet pressed against her sensitive clit.

A soft moan escaped her. "Devin." She bit her bottom lip, sucking it into her hot mouth. "I'm so close."

"Don't worry, sugar, I'm not going anywhere." He added a second finger inside her, rubbing and tapping her G-spot in an unhurried rhythm.

"More. Harder."

Eager to watch her come apart, he followed direction, ignoring the electric sensations tightening his balls. Moaning in appreciation, she rocked against his hand, riding him. He took a nipple in his mouth, pulling at it while increasing the rhythm against her clit. She cried his name as her walls tightened around his fingers. Her body arched and shook.

At length, her eyes flicked open and a lazy grin curled her mouth. She continued to stroke him, increasing the pressure and pace with each pass. "Come for me, Devin."

The buzzing in his balls reached a fevered pitch and they pulled close to the base of his cock. His hand covered hers and he tried to aim away from her, but she kept his dick pointed straight at her tits. "Ryder, I'm going to—"

"I know." She twisted her wrist on the downward stroke. "Come. For. Me."

Unable to deny her order, he surrendered to the vibrations building in his balls. The sensation intensified, stoking his pulse until the orgasm spurted from him all over her perfect tits.

Chest heaving, he leaned down and covered her mouth with his, claiming her—and that's exactly what this was. She was his now, whether she realized it or not.

# Chapter Thirteen

*"Fashion is never in crisis because clothes are always necessary."*

— *Achille Maramotti*

Ryder's eyes snapped open as the sound of a gong reverberated against her skull. Her phone vibrated just out of reach, notifying her of a text and then going silent.

Sated down to the depths of her soul, she considered ignoring the message. Devin snored beside her, oblivious to the noise. His brightly tattooed arm encircled her waist, holding her close. A rock was trying to fuse itself to her shoulder blade, or at least that's what it felt like, but it had been there most of the night. Early morning light illuminated the tent's interior, falling on her panties that had landed near the zipped closed front flap and Devin's boxers still tangled inside his pants on the floor.

The gong sounded again.

"You gonna get that?" Devin's voice, thick with sleep, brushed against her hair.

If she did, it meant she'd be letting the rest of the world into their tent haven. She'd have to leave his embrace and get dressed. They'd have to go find Sarah Molina and the money. Then they'd jet off the island and return home to Harbor City where they'd go their separate ways.

Which is exactly what she wanted.

So why was she ignoring her stupid phone as it *gong*ed a third time?

"If you don't answer it, they'll just keep calling." He punctuated his words with a kiss to the curve of her neck.

"God, I hate it when you're right." She swiped her phone off the floor and glanced at the screen. The clock read FIVE-TWENTY-EIGHT as she tapped the text message icon.

CARLOS: SM's GPS WENT ON THIS MORNING. SHE'S ON THE MOVE HEADING TOWARD AC. BONUS, I INTERCEPTED A TEXT SHE SENT. ALL IT SAID WAS: EIGHT EARL GRAY. THAT MEAN ANYTHING TO YOU?

Earl Gray. The name sparked something in Ryder's brain, but not enough. Closing her eyes, she blocked out the tent, Devin's warm body so close to her, and the lingering citrusy hint of his cologne. Her eyes snapped open. *That's it.* Smell. Tea Time smelled just like a freshly brewed pot of Earl Gray tea. Eight had to be eight o'clock.

She rolled over and grabbed Devin's face between her hands. "We've got her."

The contact sent a frisson of awareness skittering up her arm and she shivered. The shimmy drew his attention. His pupils dilated and his gaze locked on her mouth. She meant the kiss to be celebratory, but all it took was the touch of his lips to hers for the world to go off kilter again. Desire as strong as a lifelong hunger roared to the forefront and she wrapped her legs around his bare hips and twisted, flipping him onto his back. Holding his arms above his head, she kissed her way down his neck and sucked on his collarbone.

"Damn, you taste good first thing in the morning." She licked along the bright purple curve of the tribal tattoo on his right pec. Her hand slithered down between their bodies to grasp his hard-on. "I could eat you right up—if there was time."

"I just knew there had to be a catch."

"Always." She gave him a hard, quick kiss as the day's details worked themselves out in her head. "You know it's probably a trap."

"She hasn't exactly been trying to cover her tracks."

"True." Ryder weighed the options. Follow the coordinates and risk walking into a worse shit storm than they were in already? It sure as hell sounded like suicide. Then again, Sarah had a gift for hiding right out in the open, so there was no guarantee they'd get this close again before the merger deadline. "Sarah's smart and she's been onto us from the get-go, but it's our best worst chance."

Working alone, Ryder had a slim chance of success. Her gaze slid over to the half-naked man beside her. But together? If it was a trap, she had to make sure Devin made it out with enough time to call in her brother and the cavalry.

They had the where and the when. If they kept it simple—and didn't get themselves killed—Sarah could fall right in their laps. They'd have her on the jet with the wheels up before her thugs even realized what had happened.

"You have good instincts, I trust you." Devin tucked a hair behind her ear. "You should, too."

Bounding up from his warmth before she got lost in him again, she slipped on her panties, washed her chest, and tossed Devin his clothes. "Get a move on, stud. I've got a plan."

• • •

Ryder stifled a yawn as the early morning sunrays broke over the single-story roofs of Andol City's downtown, and did her best to ignore the funky scent emanating from the nearby overflowing trash barrels. While she was at it, she kept her gaze averted from the man with smoke pouring from his ears beside her. Let him stew, her plan was solid. All he had to do was follow her lead and they'd be golden.

Devin crossed his arms as the Jeep's engine idled in an alley just off the central square. "I don't like this. I should be by your side."

"Which you've made abundantly clear." She opened the passenger door, ready to hop down to the fast-warming asphalt. "But there are only two entry points for Tea Time. She's either going in the front or hitting it from the back door, which we can't see from this standpoint."

"I don't want you out of my sight." His aviator sunglasses hid his eyes, but he couldn't cover up the vein throbbing in his temple.

*Saints preserve her from overprotective men.* "Can the he-man bullshit. I'm a professional."

"It all changed last night." He kept his profile to her, but reached out to intertwine his fingers with hers. "Things are different now."

"Not my ability to do my job." His concern flattered and annoyed her even as the simple act of holding hands left her aching for more of him. And wasn't that complication just par for the course when it came to this man? "Trust me. The plan will work."

"What if Sarah doesn't show?"

"She'll be there." She had to be, otherwise their chances of success within the designated time frame went from slim to microscopic. Not something Ryder wanted to think about. "See you soon."

Abandoning the Jeep and the pissed off man behind

the wheel, she loped down the alley toward a six-foot-high concrete pineapple in front of a jewelry store. Without slowing her pace, she scrambled up to the statue's pointy top and leaped from it to the building's roof. Setting up in the shadow of a rooftop air conditioner, she hunkered down for what she hoped would be a short wait. From her perch, she had an unobstructed view of Tea Time's back door and the police headquarters—for all the good proximity to Andol City's version of law and order would do them. Shit, with the crooked cops sitting inside, having them so close would probably do more to hurt them.

She glanced at her watch. *Half past seven.* If everything was going according to schedule, Devin had ditched the hot pink Jeep in a municipal lot by now and was on his way up the wooden staircase to the rooftop garden on top of the sidewalk café across from Tea Time. She craned her neck and scanned the shadows surrounding the café's potted palms and brightly colored hanging plants, but came up empty. Then an early morning sun ray hit a reflective surface, making it look as though the shadows were winking.

*Devin's aviators.* Had to be.

Everything was in place—everything except Sarah Molina. As the minutes ticked by, tourists on mopeds and locals in compact cars and four-wheel drives cruised down Main Street. The bakery down the street turned over its open sign and employees filtered into other businesses surrounding the tea shop.

Ryder chewed the inside of her check, trying to burn off the fidgety energy coursing through her. *Seven fifty-eight.* From the information she'd gathered, Sarah Molina had lived her life at Dylan's Department Store like a drill sergeant. *If you weren't early, you were late*, according to the domineering executive assistant. But she chose now to break her own rule? Odd didn't begin to cover the creepy-crawly feeling dancing up Ryder's spine.

When eight o'clock rolled around, most of the businesses lining Main Street had opened, but the tea shop stayed dark and no one approached the building.

Her stomach folded in on itself as she searched the streets for any sign of Sarah or a mysterious buyer. This couldn't be happening.

*Eight-fifteen.*

She'd missed something, Ryder felt it in her bones. What it was, she had no fucking clue.

She searched the area for the reflection from Devin's sunglasses and came up empty.

Her mind spinning through the possibilities, she loped to the alley side of the building and scurried down the drainpipe. Halfway down, her thumb snagged on a metal brace securing the pipe to the turquoise-painted cement wall. Pain shot up her arm and she lost her grasp on the metal. She dropped the final few feet to the ground. Her thumb throbbed and there was a slice of skin missing, but nothing that wouldn't heal. Just like the other bazillion scrapes and bruises from yesterday's fight. She sucked on the side of her thumb, the metallic flavor of her blood tasting a lot like defeat.

But there wasn't time to whine about it now. She had to find Devin. Taking off at a quick jog down the alley toward the Jeep, she kept to the building's shadows and collided with a rail-thin tabby cat tearing around the corner. It bounced off her shins and continued along the alley as if a pack of wild dogs were on its tail.

Ryder's sixth sense electrified the hair on the back of her neck and she slowed her pace. Approaching the end of the building with caution, she peeked around the corner at the now bustling Main Street. Shoppers shuffled down the sidewalks, stopping every few feet to look in a store window. Cars and mopeds puttered down the main drag, many circling the square at a crawl, trolling for a parking spot. Even the birds chirped as if all was right in the world.

Ready to sprint out into the street, she spotted a tell-tale reflection. She peered closer and spied the outline of Devin's buzz cut hair. Relief took the starch out of her spine.

Still, she couldn't shake the feeling something was off. It scratched against her skin like a stiff tag on a new shirt.

That's when she spotted a woman with a glossy ebony bob in the window of the coffee shop and bakery across the street from Tea Time. A couple of lowlifes loitered outside the glass front doors. Ryder narrowed her gaze. The woman turned her head so she faced the street and took off a pair of oversize white Chanel sunglasses. *Bingo*.

Ryder whipped out her phone, accessed the camera, and zoomed in. The picture was fuzzy, but confirmed it was Sarah Molina.

The woman had elephant-sized brass balls to hang out in plain sight with only a pair of lackeys as protection. The goons in question were more interested in flinging rocks at the island cats roaming the streets than keeping an eye out for trouble.

Ryder was scanning the perimeter, searching for a secondary entry and exit point to the bakery when a dark blue, older model van slowed in front of the café and the side door slid open. The guards dropped their handfuls of pebbles and hustled into the vehicle. The van burned rubber as it pulled away from the curb, leaving Sarah on her own.

Okay. That should make the grab and dash a little easier. There might be more goons inside the bakery, but Ryder wouldn't know until she got closer.

*This was her chance*. Adrenaline pumped through her veins, sharpening her focus. She glanced up at the rooftop garden above the bakery, grabbed her phone, and dialed Devin's number. "She's in the bakery across the street."

"What the fuck is she doing there?"

Sarah sipped from a mint-green cup as if she didn't have a care in the world.

"Maybe she's sneaking a cup of coffee instead of tea." Ryder stayed out of Sarah's line of sight as she crossed the bustling street and made her way toward the bakery.

"I'm on my way down." The sound of Devin's feet thumping across the roof echoed over the phone line.

"No, Devin. You get the Jeep." She paused at the corner of the bakery, her back flat against the cement wall so she couldn't be seen from the window. "I'll grab her and meet you out front. Then we'll blaze a trail for the airport. Alert the jet to be ready to take off."

"I don't like it."

"You don't have to. You just have to trust me to know how to do my job. Be out front in three minutes."

"Ryder—"

She clicked off her phone, more than finished with that conversation, and kept her face averted as she strode toward the door as if nothing in the world was the matter. After two years of following cheating husbands and sneaking wives, she knew the drill well. Skulkers drew attention. People who acted like they belonged somewhere blended into the scenery.

Angling her body so her face couldn't be seen and inhaling a deep breath, she reached for the bakery door handle.

The screech of brakes sounded behind her. Ryder didn't have to look back to know trouble had arrived. In the front door's reflection, she spotted the dark blue van with a bruised up Long Hair in the driver's seat and Freckles riding shotgun. She watched them with a muttered curse, but something else had captured their attention.

"*Americano*." Freckles pointed down the street.

She turned in time to see the hot pink Jeep peel around the corner, heading straight for them.

The bakery door opened behind her.

The Jeep squealed to a stop.

Behind the wheel, Devin's eyes rounded. "Ryder!"

In the next instant, everything went black.

• • •

Devin's throat closed as Ryder crumpled to the ground in front of the bakery and lay unmoving. They'd gambled and lost on whether Sarah had laid a trap, but the payment was more than he was willing to give. Adrenaline hit his blood stream at one hundred proof.

One of the Molinas' gorillas loomed over her, holding a broken ceramic cat in his right hand. Devin didn't think, he didn't consider, he just knew. He was going to kill that man. Slowly.

Powered by blood-boiling rage, he shot out of the Jeep. His only aim was to destroy everything within reach and get to Ryder.

Men poured out of the van like rats escaping a sinking ship. Most were bruised and battered from the day before. Each looked more than ready to even the score. Devin didn't give a shit. Pulling Ryder out of this shit storm and getting her on the jet was all that mattered.

He executed a hammerfist punch, connecting with a long-haired guy's jaw. The crunch of breaking bone fed the flame of fury inside him. He wheeled around, executing a chest-high side kick that planted his boot against the second thug's sternum.

After that, it was just a maelstrom of jabs, kicks, and punches. Each was meant to inflict the most severe pain possible and clear a path to Ryder.

He got within arm's reach of her when a forearm as thick as a redwood wrapped around his neck. In the next heartbeat, only his tiptoes touched the pavement.

He landed an elbow to the man's solar plexus. Air wheezed out of the giant, but his grip stayed true. Smelling blood in the water, the other goons circled closer. The cocky looks on their faces showed they thought they'd already had this thing won.

They were wrong.

Back in his mixed martial arts days, the fights were hard, but they were one-on-one. The odds were majorly against him now, but what was on the line mattered a hell of a lot more to him than a champion's belt.

Blackness danced around the edges of his vision. He had to get out of this choke hold or he'd never get to her.

Tucking his chin into the crook of the goon's arm, Devin raised his shoulders and jerked his chin into his attacker's forearm. The pressure loosened. Air whooshed into his lungs. He dropped enough for his feet to touch the ground. Immediately, he delivered a chop punch to the asshole's groin and twisted. He burst from the thug's deadly hold.

In that single moment of clarity, he fell back to his MMA mantra: *focus, finesse, fight*.

Eight guys on their feet, two on the ground, and one too busy holding his smashed nut sack to be of much trouble. A glimmer caught his eye. Sarah stood behind one of the thugs.

Understanding whacked him in the face.

*Cut off the head and kill the snake.*

Using reserves he didn't realize he had, Devin pivoted away from Ryder and plowed through a freckle-faced goon like a three-hundred-pounder versus a bag of chips. Grabbing Sarah's arm, he pulled her close so she stood between him and the pack of enforcers. He slid his other arm around her throat, ready to snap it clean in half.

"Long time no see, Sarah."

Taken by surprise, she didn't even try to break free. "I

suppose you think this is the optimum solution?"

"Returning the money is your best option." He softened his tone, hoping to remind her of the easy working relationship they'd had for the past ten years. "You return the money, we leave. No authorities get involved. You don't serve time."

"Jail? Are you kidding? Did you know George and I met on Andol? My father told me he'd disown me if I left with George. I was young and did it anyway. I gave George my undying loyalty and he repaid me by hiring a flighty nincompoop in a short skirt. I made him pay, and he'll keep paying when the MultiCorp deal falls through. It's past time for me to get my due, and no one's taking it from me."

One of the thugs grabbed Ryder. She was awake, but groggy.

Devin wanted to pluck out the guy's eyeballs and grill them on a skewer. But action without the benefit of thinking first had never turned out well for him. That's how James had ended up as he had. Devin couldn't risk hurting Ryder any more than he already had by dragging her into this mess. He had to protect her.

She blinked unfocused eyes and feebly pushed away the guy's arm, but it didn't move an inch. A crowd of tourists watched from a safe distance while the locals, on the other hand, kept their gaze purposefully averted. There wasn't a cop in sight. Naturally.

He had to play this just right or it would go sideways. That couldn't happen.

"Tell your little army to let her go."

"No." Sarah sounded as bored as if he'd asked her about the weather.

He tightened his grip around her neck. "Let. Her. Go."

"Oh, I would if it was just me, but my son is quite particular about his reputation." She shrugged. "You two caught him flat-footed with the diamonds-in-the-tea-pots scheme. It would be bad form to let both of you go."

There it was. The out he'd been looking for. "Fine. Leave her. Take me."

Sarah *tsk-tsk*ed and shook her head. "Ah, self-sacrifice. I know that stage of love all too well. It's not the most comfortable place, is it?"

His gut screamed for him to pull out all the stops and go full-on crazy, but he couldn't. The only way he'd get Ryder out of here was if he used his brain instead of his brawn.

He released Sarah. "Let her go and I'll go willingly. Maybe my father will pay a ransom." He shrugged.

Sarah, well aware of the billions his father had in the bank, considered him for a moment. "But your father hates you."

"He does, but he hates looking weak even more." Letting kidnappers keep his first born would do just that.

"Get him in the van." Sarah glanced at Ryder, who was still fighting weakly against her captor, then back at him. "Leave her."

Relief seeped into his marrow. He had no fucking clue what would happen to him next, but he imagined it would be painful and prolonged. It didn't matter, as long as Ryder was safe.

Two of the men grabbed his arms, shoved him into the vehicle, and tied him to one of the seats.

As the van doors slid closed, the last thing he saw was Ryder sinking to the ground.

# Chapter Fourteen

*"You can be anyone you want to be, with the right outfit."*

— *Melody Minagar*

Ryder cracked open her eyelids and light pierced through her eyes like a shiv, jabbing into her pounding brain. Reflexively, she squeezed them shut again and tried to process the anxiety chewing a hole in her stomach. Her memory of how she'd gotten here, and where exactly here was, was a jumbled mess. The last thing she remembered was the blue van pulling up, followed by the Jeep and—

*Devin.*

Her breath caught as a hot flash of fear razed what was left of the haze fogging up her thinking. Had he made it to the bakery? Did the Molinas have him, too? She'd asked him to trust her judgment and he had. *Fuck.*

That decision may have cost him his life—or at the very

least his freedom, and possibly a whole lot of pain.

Finding him wasn't an option. It was *the only* option.

While it may be warranted, panicking wasn't going to do shit to get either of them out of this situation. Without opening her eyes, she took in a deep breath and used her other senses to gather intel and figure out where in the hell she was. She didn't dare let on she was awake, in case she was being watched. Crisp sheets and a soft mattress lay beneath her. Salty air wafted in from the left. The quiet *click* of a door shutting broke the perfect silence. In or out? Best to bet on in and act accordingly.

A squinty-eyed peek confirmed she wasn't outside the bakery anymore. She was in the suite at the Palm Inn.

Soft footsteps sounded behind her, setting off her internal alarms.

If the Molinas were planning to kill her, she sure as hell wasn't about to make it easy for them. She visualized the room, searching her memory for a weapon.

She rolled to her side facing away from the door and wrapped her fingers around the bedside lamp's solid brass base. In one fluid motion, she sat up, twisted, and brought the lamp down toward the approaching target.

"Oh good, you're awake—" Borja's greeting ended in a squawk.

She stopped the lamp's downward path inches from his black hair. "Where's Devin?" she demanded. Her chest heaved, not with exertion but with the desperate, aching need to know. She couldn't attribute that kind of physical reaction to a missing client.

Devin had become much more than a mere client, well before she'd ever had the good sense to realize it...because she'd been too caught up in constantly proving what a badass she was.

Borja held his hands up, palms out. "Everything will be

fine. The Molinas are nowhere near here. You're safe with us."

"Where is he?" she asked again.

"I do not have good news on that front." Borja took several steps back from the bed, his gaze locked on the heavy lamp in her hand. "He is alive—at least he was when he got in the van. But the Molinas have him."

Ryder jackknifed off the bed, intent on finding Devin. But the room swum before her and the lamp fell from her grasp. The throbbing in her head intensified, rattling her molars. Borja's hand on her shoulder gently pushed her back down to the mattress before her knees gave way.

"Take these." The hotel manager held out two white pills and a glass of clear liquid.

She pushed his hand away. "Forget it. I remember what happened last time I had something to drink here."

"What do you...? Ah, the wine. It is particularly potent. But this is plain water and aspirin. I promise."

"Potent? It was drugged."

"Oh, Mama likes to talk about its mystical powers, but it's just home-brewed wine that's fermented too long. It always gives me the worst headaches. Speaking of which—" He dropped the aspirin in her hand and held out the water glass. "Take this, it will help."

The pills carried the markings of a major pharmaceutical company on one side and the word aspirin stamped on the other. She sniffed the liquid. If it was drugged, it was unscented. "Why are you helping me?"

"Not everyone on the island is happy with how things work in Andol City." He shrugged. "We do what we can."

His tone was as easy as if she'd asked about that night's dinner special, but his nostrils flared with emotion.

"What have they done to you?" she asked, sensing there was a story there, and not a good one.

A dark shadow crossed Borja's face and his jaw tightened.

"You notice I have my mother here, but not my father."

"I'm sorry."

"I was twelve. They kept Mama for three weeks before we could scrape together enough money to pay the ransom."

Ryder couldn't miss the raw pain that deepened each one of the lines dividing his forehead before he looked to his feet, blinking rapidly. Better not to go there. But that look did not bode well for anyone they'd kidnapped.

She popped the aspirin in her mouth and swallowed a mouthful of water. "Do you know where they're holding Devin?"

"I imagine he's at their farm."

Picturing the small, single-story house with its weathered appearance and lack of guards, she couldn't get it to jibe with a secure location. "The house with the pineapples out front? It didn't seem like a good spot for that."

"Oh, not there. They have a much bigger place a few miles further inland." A knock sounded at the door. "That must be your friends."

She tossed the pills in her mouth and washed them down with the water. Everything ached, but nothing hurt more than the knowledge that all of this was her fault for rushing in when she should have called for backup. She just prayed it wasn't too late for Devin. She grabbed the bedside telephone and dialed.

Her brother picked up on the second ring.

"Tony, I need you. How soon can you be here?"

Silence loud enough to break her eardrum thrummed through the line before he answered. "How soon do you need me?"

• • •

The sun had almost disappeared below the western horizon

when Maltese Security's three musketeers filed into Ryder's hotel room. Carlos shuffled in first wearing a Dr. Who T-shirt, jeans cuffed at the ankles, and a commiserating grimace. Cam strutted in next. They had to have been airborne for nearly ten hours, yet he looked like he'd just walked off a magazine cover with his glossy hair and almost too pretty face. He gave Ryder a quick wink and a thumbs up.

Her big brother marched in last, looking about as happy as a vegetarian at a North Carolina barbecue where greens fried in bacon fat was the only non-meat option.

Ryder held up her hand before Tony could open his mouth. "You're right and, yes, I need your help."

All three men stopped in their tracks.

Cam was the first to recover. "Who are you, and what've you done with Ryder?"

She rolled her eyes. "Stuff it, Cam."

"That's more like the Ryder I know and love." He flashed his signature wicked grin.

"The Molinas have taken Devin captive." Just saying the words made her stomach cramp, the perfect accompaniment to the dull pounding of her head and the ache in her chest no amount of medicine could dull. "I can't get him back without your help."

She gulped around the rock lodged deep in her throat and glanced down at her matching bracelet of interwoven gold threads and recalled the feel of his strong hands on her foot during their plane ride to The Andol Republic. His touch had been the only thing keeping her sane when her fear of flying had gone into the danger zone. And at their blessing ceremony, his nearness had kept her from running away in a panic. Even this morning, when he'd been annoyed as all hell and thinking her plan was nuts, he'd trusted her.

The realization landed like an elephant on her chest. She couldn't lose him now. He meant too much to her.

Carlos sat down at the small hotel room desk and took out his laptop. Used to his quirks, Ryder didn't think twice when he kept his gaze glued to his screen and his fingers busy on the keyboard while she quickly went through everything that had happened since she and Devin arrived two days ago. Well, almost everything. She never mentioned the blessing ceremony and Borja didn't speak up, thank God, but she couldn't stop touching the golden bracelet as if it really tied her to Devin.

"Any proof that he's still on the island…or alive?" The blunt question marked the first time Tony had spoken since entering.

She shook her head, not even wanting to think about the second possibility. "Only my gut."

"No offense, girlie"—Cam sat down on the bed next to her—"but that's not much to go on."

"If I may." Borja stepped forward. "I was just telling Ms. Falcon earlier that the family has a large warehouse on their farm."

Cam quirked an eyebrow at the manager's formal use of her name, but kept his smart mouth shut for once.

Carlos didn't bother to look up from his laptop. "I brought up the farm on satellite the other day. There is a large building about three miles from the house."

"I never saw that image," Ryder said, annoyed.

"That's because you took off half-cocked before I got all the intel to you."

"Sorry."

"Yeah, well don't do it again." Carlos' fingers flew across the keyboard. "I'm bringing the images up now. Looks like there's just one road leading into the property. It's all flat grassland with no cover in any direction. We'd need an invisibility cloak to get in without giving them at least a twenty minute heads up to our approach. But that's not the worst of it. They have a small runway and the warehouse is big enough to house a prop plane."

"So they can fly on out at any time. That sucks," Cam muttered. "How are the authorities here?"

Ryder snorted. "Complicit or afraid."

"Let me work on backup." Cam strolled to the corner and started working his charm on whoever was lucky enough to pick up the other end of his phone call.

Borja cleared his throat and backed to the door. "If you'll excuse me, I must make a telephone call." He slipped out without waiting for a response.

"Is he safe?" Tony's voice held a mercenary edge that sent a shiver down her spine.

She traced her thumb across the rope bracelet, certainty calming her nerves. "Yes."

"Fine. Are you good enough to get off that bed? We need to talk." He strode out onto the patio, sitting down at the table where she'd had breakfast with Devin only the day before.

Planting her feet on the floor, she stood slowly and took in a calming breath. The room didn't spin and her head didn't explode. It may not be much, but it was progress and she'd take what she could get. She had to. Devin didn't have time for her to stop and whine about her probable-concussion aftereffects. Cam gave her another thumbs up while Carlos never looked up from his screen.

She stepped outside and shut the sliding door behind her. A warm breeze lifted her hair, making it dance along her skin, reminding her of Devin's touch.

"Just what in the fuck do you think you were doing?" Her brother's angry voice jarred her back to the present. "You were supposed to find an embezzler. Then you leave the country with some harebrained plan to go kidnap someone from a foreign country like some kind of rogue CIA agent in a bad movie. Jesus, Ryder, you didn't even send me a text until you were already on the plane."

He wasn't saying anything she hadn't already told herself, but still her hackles went up. Old habits died hard. "I'm not a complete idiot, Tony. I am capable of running a case."

"I know that, and if you actually ever tried to do something by the book as a team instead of constantly going off on your own and playing by your own rule book, I'd be more than happy to put you on your own cases. Lord knows it would benefit the business."

She blinked and looked, really looked, at her brother. He had dark circles under his eyes and a weariness that she realized had been there for the past few months. "What are you talking about?"

"You think I've kept you on cheating spouses cases because I thought you were incompetent? Shit, if that was the case I would have fired you, sister or not." He shoved a hand through his thick hair and sighed. "I never doubted your ability. Whenever it counts, you're always point on."

A list of mistakes ran through her mind longer than the end movie credits. "Not always."

"I know about Heath." The vein in Tony's temple throbbed.

Surprise emptied out nearly every thought in her head but one. "How?"

"Sylvie." He shrugged. "She was so mad, she wanted to burn down the world looking for him, and after she told me what happened, so did I." He held up his hand. "Don't worry, once we find him, you'll get first crack at his melon. But you can't lose your trust in yourself because of him. Don't give him that power."

That's when it hit her. It wasn't her judgment on the job that was most important. Heath hadn't only lied to her and hurt her, he'd made her question her own instincts when it came to life, to the people she cared about, to what really mattered. But not anymore.

Fear for Devin one-two punched her hard. "Devin's not just a client."

"What do you—" He slumped back against the metal chair. "Shit, Ryder, when did this happen? You've only known him for what, a week?"

"We knew each other before this." She blinked back emotion.

Their first night together seemed like a lifetime ago, but somehow she'd known even then that Devin was different. Which was why she'd run as fast as she could…only to end up right back smack dab in the middle of a bed with him again. The sex was great, but it wasn't just that. It never had been all about the sex. What exactly it was about him that spoke to her, she couldn't deal with thinking about right now. That would have to wait until they got him back safely.

"Tony, I'll do whatever it takes to make sure Devin's safe." She bit the inside of her cheek and held her breath to keep tears from falling.

Tony shook his head, reached across the table, and covered her hand with his. "We'll get him. I swear." He leaned back. "Now, I need some food so we can put together a plan. How's room service in this joint?"

# Chapter Fifteen

*"Fashion is not frivolous. It is a part of being alive today."*

— *Mary Quant*

Ryder looked longingly at the puddle of black clothes in the bathroom's corner as she fingered the soft pink sarong similar to the one she'd worn for the blessing ceremony. Her gold rope bracelet slid down her forearm as she reached up to twist a length of hair, but her fingers came up empty. Long stray strands of hair littered the floor, a ten-inch long chunk of brown hair held together by a rubber band lay on the counter. Instead of tangling around her shoulders, the curls stopped at her chin. The temporary dye job had turned the color to an almost blue black. At least the ebony color was as familiar as her all-black wardrobe since everything thing else reflected in the mirror was so different—not bad, but unfamiliar.

Maybe it was time for that.

She didn't know if this crazy scheme would work, but when Borja had proposed sneaking into the Molina warehouse under the guise of a De Mis Promesas festival delegation, it was the best bad idea they had. And if it didn't work, they'd have to pray that Cam's calls to some mysterious buddies in Chile panned out, because Ryder was *not* leaving Devin in the Molinas' clutches any longer.

Taking a deep breath, she squared her shoulders and pulled open the bathroom door.

"There is no way this will work." Ever since she'd gone in to change thirty minutes ago, Cam had been arguing they should wait for a call back from his friends before moving on the warehouse. "No one can miss Ryder in a crowd. Face it, the girl in black always stands out."

She cleared her throat and the four men turned. And blinked. A lot.

"You look...different," Carlos squeaked, before Cam jammed an elbow into his side.

An uncharacteristic blush burned her cheeks. "As long as we get Devin out of there, it doesn't matter how I look."

"My sisters have agreed to include you in the delegation, but I cannot guarantee your success." Borja rolled to the balls of his feet and clasped his hands behind his back. "The guards may not allow you on the property."

She clutched her fist to her hollow stomach before she could stop herself. Pinching her lips together until the insides cut on her teeth, she forced herself back from panic's edge. Rolling her neck from side to side, she loosened her shoulders. Just as before a match, she pushed her doubts and negativity into a deep, dark, shadowy place in her brain and locked a mental door. She refused to think about the possibility of failure. Because this wasn't just a meaningless sparring match. This was Devin's life.

"And your sisters and their friends know to get the hell

out of there if things go south?" Tony asked.

"If by 'south' you mean if everything goes wrong, then yes, they are aware that they should not stick around."

Tony clapped Borja on the shoulder. "Perfect."

"Thank you for doing this, Borja." She gave the man a quick hug.

"It is past time we stood up to them." He clenched his teeth and looked off into the distance. "Past time."

Cam's phone rang. "Yo, Bolton. What's the word?" He nodded and gave the room a thumbs up. "You got clearance from the president himself to clean up our little mess? Damn, you do have deep connections. Thanks man."

Ryder looked around at the little band of gorilla warriors. The hotel manager with a grudge. The computer geek with his military-grade, practically-unbreakable laptop and communications gear strapped to his back. The pretty boy fighter with friends who cleaned up violent messes. And her big brother protecting her back, not because he didn't think she could do the job but because he knew she could.

The sight was humbling enough to make her bottom lip quake.

Tony cocked his head and gave her a questioning look. "So we're a go?

Shaking off the emotions that had no place in the hours ahead, Ryder nodded her head. "Let's do this."

. . .

The rope burned against Devin's wrists as he twisted his arms in an attempt to reach the knot with his fingers. If he could reach the damn thing, he'd have a chance to work it free. If nothing else, he might be able to pull the bonds loose enough to slip a hand free. Unfortunately, the hours he'd been out cold tied to the chair with his arms behind his back had left his fingers numb and bordering on useless.

He'd bought Ryder time by going with Sarah, but he doubted she'd make it off the island without the Molinas taking their pound of flesh. That was, if she'd even leave. The woman was as stubborn as the day was long, and he couldn't quite convince himself that she'd make the calculated move to get the hell away from The Andol Republic without him.

Not that he totally hated the idea, even though he should. Her badass attitude was one of the things that had sucked him into her orbit like a planet around a star. That, and her phenomenal ass.

The image of her high, round ass added to his motivation as he flexed his wrists and stretched his fingers as far as they could go. The tip of his pointer finger brushed the knot's scratchy surface. Inching it across the curve, he tried to nudge the rope from where it was twisted into itself. It didn't budge, and he wanted to roar out his frustration. Instead, he swallowed the noise, not wanting to draw his guards' attention. The last time he'd done that, he'd lost at least an hour and what felt like a pint of blood acting as their personal punching bag. If he was going to get out of here—and he *was*—he had to use his head instead of his biceps, or his big mouth.

Concentrating all of his energy on getting at the knot, he reached again with everything he had. The rope shifted and gave a few millimeters. His pulse punched into overdrive.

A shout in Spanish from the other side of the closed door halted his forward progress as he strained to pick up a word or two and translate them in his head.

Stop.

Festival.

Pineapple.

Girls.

Beautiful.

Then male laughter, full of bravado and innuendo.

A minute later, female voices joined the deeper ones.

A booty call? Now? Clearly, they weren't the least bit worried about him.

Devin moved his fingers faster. This could be the perfect opportunity. If he could just loosen his bounds, the guards might be distracted by the women long enough for him to make a dash for it.

The knot slipped. He turned his wrists more and flexed his hands until the rope fell. Blood rushed into his fingers like a bullet train full of oh-fuck-that-hurts burning its way through his veins. It stung like a son of a bitch, but he pushed past the pain and bent over to untie his ankles. At least his guards hadn't used duct tape.

He stood, pins and needles streaking down his legs, and looked for a weapon in the small, dusty storage room. There were a few wooden crates, but the guards had taken the crowbars and other tools with them.

The doorknob jiggled.

He had half a heartbeat to make a decision.

He grabbed one of the smaller crates—which still weighed about forty pounds—and stood behind the door so it would block him from view when it opened.

The knob turned.

Centering his stance, he lifted the crate above his head as high as he could, his arms screaming in protest.

One of the guards and a short-haired woman in pink sashayed into the room, arm in arm. He couldn't see her face, but he didn't give a damn who it was. He just needed the perfect shot at the guard's head.

On a jetted exhale, Devin brought the crate down, knocking the man out cold and pushing the woman to the side. Without pausing for a breath, he kicked the door shut, grabbed the woman, and slapped a hand over her mouth.

She squirmed against him, trying her damnedest to land

an elbow or crack the back of her skull against his face.

"Look lady, I'm not going to—" That was all he got out before her heel slammed into his instep.

White hot pain shot up his leg. His palm on her lips faltered for a second, but he managed to keep his grip around her waist. He pulled her close so that her back lay flat against his chest and her short, dark curly hair tickled his cheek. The scent of cinnamon hiding in her ebony hair made his brain hiccup.

She took advantage of the momentary lapse to bite down on his hand hard enough that he reflexively whipped it away from her.

"I'm here to rescue you, you idiot." She went limp in his arms. A move that would have made someone less familiar with fighting tactics drop her on her ass.

As he tightened his grip, his mind tried to put the sound of that voice together with the stranger swathed in the pink, filmy dress standing snug up against him. Luckily, his body immediately recognized that toned, curvy flesh, even if his brain didn't. "*Ryder?*"

"Yes. Now let me go. We don't have a ton of time."

"What the hell are you doing here? You should be gone. It's too dangerous. I have to protect you."

"No." She shook her head. "You don't fight for me. We fight for each other."

The truth of the statement knocked the heavy weight from his shoulders and he couldn't find the words to express the lightness and certainty that she was right.

"How many times did they whack you in the head?" She whirled in his arms, grabbed his face between her palms, and stared hard into his eyes, presumably searching for signs of brain damage. "What day is it? Who's president?"

"They whacked me plenty." Not that he was feeling anything other than awareness now that the feel of her skipped up his skin. "But I'm pretty hard-headed."

His answer must have satisfied her because she dropped her hands to her sides, though she winced at his new cuts and bruises. "I feel your pain." She knelt down, flipped the passed out guard onto his back, and shoved her hands into his pockets. "Yes!" She yanked a set of keys out of one.

"That's your plan? We jack his car and just drive out of here?"

She jumped to her feet, cocked a hip, and stared him down. "You got a better idea?"

He considered the ten thick-necked muscle men on the other side of the door, the firepower each carried, and calculated the chances they'd actually make it out unharmed. Talk about a clusterfuck. He opened his mouth to say so when Ryder quirked an eyebrow at him, practically daring him to disregard her ability to get the job done. And he realized he didn't. If she said this was the best option, it was.

He shook his head. "Fresh out."

"Okay, then. Let's go." She reached for the door.

"Wait." He grabbed her wrist, his thumb sliding across her gold bracelet, yanked her close, and crushed her mouth with his. It wasn't their first kiss, and he hoped like hell it wasn't their last, but he meant for it to be a damned memorable one. He put everything he had into it, all the wanting, all the needing, and all the ever after—if they were lucky enough to have one, and he sure as hell hoped they were.

She pulled away thirty seconds later with swollen lips and a dazed look in her dark brown eyes. "You'd better be following that up later."

"It's a date." The caveman in him beat his chest. "Now, let's get out of here."

She yanked open the door and they ran out into a scene of utter chaos as the guards scattered and a group of women fled out the front door.

• • •

A *whoomp, whoomp, whoomp* sounded outside the warehouse's open windows. Low-level dirt clouds whirled around Ryder's ankles as she darted out from the storage room where they'd stuffed Devin. No one gave her a first look, let alone a second glance. The guards were too busy staring out the windows as an armada of helicopters swooped down from the sky.

*Holy crap.* Ryder shook her head in wry amazement as adrenaline ricocheted through her body. "Looks like Cam's friends made it."

Guys in ninja black zipped down rope lines from the hovering helicopters, hit the ground running, and headed straight for the warehouse. Highly trained and determined, the mercenaries looked every bit as dangerous as Cam had promised they'd be.

"Shall we let them in?" Devin grinned through his bruises, obviously enjoying the ensuing chaos and hullabaloo as much as she was.

"Why not?" She took off at a sprint to the garage bay door at the front of the warehouse and hit the OPEN button. The dented metal door creaked upward.

Behind them, one of the guards yelled in Spanish.

A knife whizzed past Ryder's head, embedding itself in the wood at eye level.

Spinning around, she raised her fists so they were just below eye level.

Long Hair and Freckles stood hip-to-hip, both looking a little worse for wear from their last encounter.

"*Puta,*" Freckles snarled.

Ryder grinned behind her fists. "*Si.*" Anticipation bubbled inside her, a hunger to make these punks pay for what they'd done to Devin, and to the rest of the island.

She didn't wait for him to make a move, but claimed the

aggressor's route. Keeping her fists up, she landed her right leg with a solid *thump* right below Freckles's chest. Air wheezed out of his mouth like a popped inner tube.

From the corner of her eye, she saw Long Hair, the bulkier of the two guards, rush Devin. He shoved his shoulder into Devin's solar plexus in an attempt to knock him off balance. And failed. They jostled for control, punching and grappling. With a low growl, Devin swung out one leg and swept Long Hair off his feet.

Freckles made a half-ass punch attempt, and Ryder followed up with a fast punching combination and roundhouse kick, before grabbing his arm, spinning into position, and flipping him over in the air. A plume of dust rose when Freckles smacked down against the dirt floor.

"I'll be glad to see the last of those two once we blow this island." Devin leveled a solid kick to Long Hair's ribs.

"Amen." She headed toward the door as the mercenaries rushed in yelling for the Molina men inside to get on their knees, hands on heads. The bright late afternoon sun blazed hot overhead, temporarily blinding her, but not before she caught a glimpse of Sarah hustling around the warehouse's corner. She slammed to a stop, her mind speeding.

Devin halted beside her. "Where to?"

"Truck." She pointed to the half-rusted four-by-four parked at an angle and tossed him the keys from the jailer's pocket. "I'll be right there, I just have to grab something."

She bolted after Sarah, determination pushing her forward with each stride. She almost caught up with the embezzler about a hundred yards from the warehouse, in the middle of the flat grassland leading to the volcano. Digging deep, she added an extra burst of speed—enough to reach out and grab the back of Sarah's shirt, jerking her backward. The other woman flew off her feet.

"Where exactly do you think you're going?" She twisted

her hand in Sarah's collar, pulling it taut around her neck.

"*Bitch*." Sarah spit out the word.

Ryder snorted. "That all you got?"

The older woman dug in her heels. "I'm not going with you."

"No?" Ryder dragged the other woman forward, not giving a shit about the size-five ruts she left behind in the ground. "There are some men in black who can't wait to see you."

"The Andol Republic has no extradition agreement with the United States. This is kidnapping!" Hysteria sharpened Sarah's voice.

"You should know." She hauled the struggling woman across the dirt yard in front of the warehouse. "But who said anything about the U.S.?"

"Wh—what do you mean?"

Ryder pulled to a stop in front of a man in opaque sunglasses dressed in more black than she wore on a good day. He held up a finger as he chomped on a wad of gum big enough to give every major league ballplayer a plug. Nodding, he pressed a button on his earpiece.

"Yes, sir, the location is contained. The subjects are in custody. Mission complete."

Taking a moment to relish the success, Ryder glanced back at Devin. He was leaning against the front end of the ancient truck, his ankles crossed and a shit-eating grin on his face. A shiver that had nothing to do with adrenaline made its way up her spine.

"Ma'am?" The man in black snatched her attention away from her lover.

She dragged her prisoner forward. "This is Sarah Molina, embezzler, thief, and overall awful excuse for a grandma." She turned to Sarah. "These fine gentlemen are working with the Andol government to bring down you and your entire crime-ridden family. The only place you're going is to prison, for a very, very long time."

# Chapter Sixteen

*"First rule of cleavage: It's not how low you go, but where and when you show."*

— *Elisabeth Dale*

Helicopters and small planes packed the sleepy Andol Republic airport Ryder and Devin had flown into roughly forty-eight hours ago. She tightened her grip on her stuffed overnight bag until the hard leather handle bit into her palm, trying to steady her shaky hands.

God, had it only been two days?

An hour after the raid, she was standing at the top of the old school metal stairway that had been rolled up to the Dylan's Department Store corporate jet. She paused to look back, a bittersweet smile curving her mouth as she soaked in the island's dangerous beauty for the last time. She could just pick out the tops of the three dormant volcanoes in the distance, standing proud against a soft blue sky untouched by clouds. A salty island breeze tumbled her hair, and she automatically raised her fingers to keep the short strands from sticking to her lip gloss before remembering she didn't have to anymore.

She'd shed that dead weight, leaving herself lighter. More free.

"You coming onboard or did you change your mind and decide to fly commercial?" Devin stood just inside the jet, his muscular frame taking up most of the open doorway.

Her heart did the *cha cha* at the sight of him. "Nine hours cramped in coach when I could stretch out here on a private jet? You're kidding, right?"

"Here, let me get that for you." He held out his hand for her bag and flashed a wicked grin. "I'm just being nice. I promise, I know you can hold your own."

Her stomach did that *flip flop* thing that seemed to happen whenever she was within smelling distance of his citrus cologne. "Smart-ass."

"And you like me that way." He snatched the bag from her grasp, the briefest touch of his fingers sending sparks across her skin. "Come on, I want to show you something."

She followed him through the main cabin of the jet to a door at the back. He twisted the knob and pushed open the door. Inside was giant bed covered in black silk sheets that took up almost the entirety of the small bedroom. Decadent. Delicious.

*Dangerous.*

Much like the man standing next to her who made her breath catch every time she set eyes on him.

"I figured I needed to up my game when it came to distracting you on the flight."

"Oh, really? And you figured I'd just hop in with you?" She arched an eyebrow and leaned against the bedroom wall.

"I know you have some ridiculous year-without-commitments thing going on, but I intend to devote every minute of the next nine hours convincing you that your misguided resolution is the dumbest thing on the face of the earth." He reached behind her neck and pulled the pink tie holding her sarong.

Her heart fluttered as the material slithered down her chest, snagging on her hard nipples. "Why, Mr. Harris, is that a challenge?"

"No it's the first step in my Big Plan." His finger feathered across her collarbone, coming to rest against the pulse jumping in her neck.

"World domination?" Done with his teasing, she reached for his belt, but he captured her hands and pulled her arms taut above her head. Desire pooled in her belly, hot and demanding.

"Something bigger." He lowered his lips within a hair's breadth of hers. "You're mine, Ryder. *Mine*. I just need you to agree."

Stunned, she couldn't move as his tongue teased her lips, sending heat flaring through her body. The flames burned away her resistance. Not that she had any…

"Open up for me, Ryder."

Her body vibrated at his growled command and she opened for him. One day he'd ask the question, *yeah, that question*, and she'd say yes. She knew it as surely as she knew her Nonni made the best gravy in the world and that chocolate cannoli were the only kind worth eating. But she wouldn't make it easy for him. They both enjoyed the challenge of the chase too much.

He deepened the kiss and his hands swept down her sides, coming to rest against the outside of her thighs. The sarong's filmy material teased her bare legs as he inched it higher and higher until it bunched around her waist.

The contrasting texture of his rough hands and the

smooth silk of her panties teased her desire. She buried her fingers in his thick hair, wanting to touch him everywhere at once. There wasn't her. There wasn't him. There was only *them*. She wanted what only Devin could give and she refused to live another moment without it.

Desperate for more, she pulled back from his hungry mouth, grabbed a handful of his shirt in each fist, and yanked hard. Buttons flew across the jet's small bedroom, leaving exposed his muscular chest covered in bright tattoos. She planned to spend at least an hour tracing them with her fingers and wet tongue.

"On the bed or against the wall?"

"Yes, please." The ache deep within her intensified. Her sensitive skin craved his touch, yearned for him.

His hands curved around to her ass, cupping each globe in his palms and lifting her so her yearning core fit perfectly against his hard cock. He rocked against her, and she wrapped her legs tightly around his lean waist. Wanting him. Needing him. Desperate for him.

Her lips busy with his, she spread her fingers wide and ran them across his broad shoulders, pushing his ruined shirt down his tattooed arms. His citrus cologne teased her as she followed the curve of his biceps, tensing under her touch.

Pulling her mouth away from his was torture, but it was the only way she could taste more of him and lick away the island from his warm skin. His pulse jumped against his corded neck as she trailed kisses down his throat. Pausing to tongue his hammering pulse, she relished that he wanted this as much as she did. Her quick nip elicited a harsh groan from him. Then he groaned again.

Pushing her gently backward, he framed her face with his hands, forcing her to make eye contact. All of the teasing had fled from his latte-colored gaze. Whatever he was about to say mattered.

"Say you're done with no commitments," he said intensely. Her heart tripped. "I'm done."

"Thank God." He ripped her sarong away, flipped her around, and laid her onto the silk sheets.

Anticipation fluttered through her as his hand snaked down her flat belly and sneaked under the elastic of her panties. He sank a single finger between her wet folds. Her back bowed, strung so tight with pleasure it nearly broke her.

The jet vibrated under them, picking up speed as it rushed down the runway. Eyes clenched shut, she felt a buzzing in her limbs as he stroked her clit. The hum grew in intensity when he slid first one, then two fingers inside, brushing against the sensitive cluster of nerves within. Trying to anchor herself to reality as they lifted from the ground, she reached for him.

Her fingers dug into his shoulders, but instead of bringing her back to earth, the feel of his muscles straining beneath her touch only increased her need. The vibration built deep inside her, ratcheting up with each stroke of his fingers, in and out, in and out, urgent need blinding her to any sensation but his touch. His fingers twisted within her slick core, pushing her closer and closer to release, until she shattered around him.

Panting, she rested her cheek against the cool silk sheet, not yet sated. Not by a long shot. "Fuck me, Devin. Now."

"I thought you'd never ask." His lips captured hers and the rest of the world ceased to exist.

The crinkle of foil being ripped open served as her only warning before he slid his rock hard cock inside her wetness. He drove deep into her heated core, filling her, completing her. She'd known it from their first night together, that he was the only man for her. She was done denying it. He was hers. She was his.

Digging her heels into the small of his back, she arched and ground her pussy against his hard cock. A thrum started deep within her, building with each deep stroke. Hot waves rippled up from her pussy. Every part of her strained toward orgasm. Close. *So close*. She swiveled her hips, bringing her clit in perfect alignment with him as he surged forward. Her nails dug into his shoulders as her body constricted and she came undone. A moment later, he drove into her one final time, and his entire body shook with the power of his orgasm.

Moments later, they rolled onto their backs, both of their chests still heaving with exertion.

"Ryder, I—"

"I know." She turned on her side and trailed her fingers across his muscular chest.

"I still want to say it." He captured her face between his palms, gentle but insistent. "I love you."

Her heart did that sideways shuffle-hop thing. "I love you, too. So fucking much."

His gaze fell to her left hand. "When we get home I'm going to—"

She covered his mouth with hers. There'd be plenty of time for promises later. Right now, they were sky-bound and he wasn't going anywhere.

She still had hours of letting him convince her.

# Acknowledgments

A huge thank you to my fabulous and fashion obsessed editor, Stephen, and my always stylish editor, Nina. You two are the dynamic duo of Killer Style. Bigs hugs to my street team, The Flynnbots, for all their support. You guys make the days spent in my yoga pants powered by coffee and chocolate totally worth it.

# About the Author

Avery Flynn has three slightly wild children, loves a hockey-addicted husband, and is desperately hoping someone invents the coffee IV drip. Find out more about Avery on her Web site (www.averyflynn.com), follow her on Twitter (@AveryFlynn), like her on her Facebook page (www.facebook.com/AveryFlynnAuthor), or friend her on her Facebook profile. Also, if you figure out how to send Oreos through the Internet, she'll be your best friend for life.

*Discover more mystery and suspense titles from
Entangled Ignite...*

## BOUND TO SERVE
a *Dangerous Liaisons* novel by Julie Castle

Condor is Delta Star's ultimate secret agent. Untouchable, unstoppable, and he always nails his targets. New field agent Bridget Jamison will stop at nothing to capture the terrorist Simon Perez. When the Delta Star Director threatens to take the case away from her, she agrees to be Condor's partner to keep her chance for justice. Now they're on a mission to infiltrate a dangerous criminal organization, and they'll have to keep their passion contained long enough not to risk their cover...and their lives.

## BRAZILIAN REVENGE
a *Brazilians* novel by Carmen Falcone

Human rights lawyer Leonardo Duarte wants to destroy Satyanna Darling, the woman who disappeared after a weekend of earth shattering sex...along with his priceless sculpture. But when he finds her in a Brazilian prison a year later he realizes she didn't act alone and blackmails her into helping him find the man behind the theft. But even while things heat up between them, secrets and mistrust threaten everything.

## AN UNTOUCHABLE CHRISTMAS
an *Untouchables* novella by Cindy Skaggs

Sofia Capri survived life as a mob wife, but living with FBI agent Logan Stone has its own challenges. Step one? Hosting his family for Christmas. Logan earned a place in Sofia's life rescuing her son and ending her mob life, but a mysterious phone call before dinner threatens the security he'd give anything to provide. When Sofia's son and Logan's nieces disappear from the festivities, the illusion of a normal Christmas shatters, hurling Sofia back into her nightmares.

*Also by Avery Flynn...*

KILLER TEMPTATION

KILLER CHARM

KILLER SEDUCTION


BETTING ON THE BILLIONAIRE

ENEMIES ON TAP

DODGING TEMPTATION

HIS UNDERCOVER PRINCESS